She headed for the door, then paused and turned back to him with those sparkling green eyes. "I have an idea. How about if when you get the okay from your grandfather I handle organizing the inside of the cabin for you?"

She walked back to him so he got the full effect of her beauty. Her flawless skin and perfect mouth. All that thick brown hair brushing her shoulders, making his hands itch to touch it.

"There's no need for you to do that."

"I know, but you rescued my son. There's no way I can repay you for that. Please let me help you."

He'd pretty much been a loner since his marriage ended. His choice. And this woman wasn't helping his solitude.

Dear Reader

This is my last book in the *Rocky Mountain Brides* series—for now anyway. So I'm happy that I was able to write Gina's story. She wasn't originally going to be my heroine, but then she came to life in her sister Lorelei's story, SINGLE DAD'S HOLIDAY WEDDING, and there was no other choice for me.

Abuse is a hard topic to discuss, and worse to live with. It's taken Gina Williams years to finally leave her situation and start over. Once settled in Destiny, Colorado, her worst fears come true when her ex-husband finds her and kidnaps her young son Zack.

My hero, loner ex-Army Master Sergeant Grady Fletcher, just happens to stumble into the situation, and can't walk away when he's asked to help. It's his Military Working Dog, Scout, who finds the boy, and refuses to leave his side until help comes.

Whether they like it or not, Grady and Gina are thrown together many more times. They each have emotional pain from their pasts, but soon they realise that leaning on each other helps the healing. It's a long road back for them, but they find strength in each other's arms.

I hope you enjoy the journey.

Patricia Thayer

HER
ROCKY MOUNTAIN
PROTECTOR

BY
PATRICIA THAYER

MILLS
BOON

First published in Great Britain 2013
by Mills & Boon, an imprint of Harlequin (UK) Limited.
Harlequin (UK) Limited, Eton House, 18-24 Paradise Road,
Richmond, Surrey TW9 1SR

© Patricia Wright 2013

ISBN: 978 0 263 23419 0

Harlequin (UK) policy is to use papers that are natural, renewable and recyclable products and made from wood grown in sustainable forests. The logging and manufacturing process conform to the legal environmental regulations of the country of origin.

Printed and bound in Great Britain
by CPI Antony Rowe, Chippenham, Wiltshire

Originally born and raised in Muncie, Indiana, **Patricia Thayer** is the second of eight children. She attended Ball State University, and soon afterwards headed West. Over the years she's made frequent visits back to the Midwest, trying to keep up with her growing family.

Patricia has called Orange County, California, home for many years. She not only enjoys the warm climate, but also the company and support of other published authors in the local writers' organisation. For the past eighteen years she has had the unwavering support and encouragement of her critique group. It's a sisterhood like no other.

When she's not working on a story, you might find her travelling the United States and Europe, taking in the scenery and doing story research while thoroughly enjoying herself, accompanied by Steve, her husband for over thirty-five years. Together, they have three grown sons and four grandsons. As she calls them: her own true-life heroes. On rare days off from writing you might catch her at Disneyland, spoiling those grandkids rotten! She also volunteers for the Grandparent Autism Network.

Patricia has written for over twenty years, and has authored more than forty-six books. She has been nominated for both a National Readers' Choice Award and the prestigious RITA® Award. Her book NOTHING SHORT OF A MIRACLE won an *RT Book Reviews* Reviewers' Choice award.

A longtime member of Romance Writers of America, she has served as President and held many other board positions for her local chapter in Orange County. She's a firm believer in giving back.

Check her website, www.patriciathayer.com, for upcoming books.

Recent books by Patricia Thayer:

SINGLE DAD'S CHRISTMAS WISH
THE COWBOY COMES HOME*
ONCE A COWBOY...**
TALL, DARK, TEXAS RANGER**
THE LONESOME RANCHER**
LITTLE COWGIRL NEEDS A MOM**

*The Larkville Legacy
**The Quilt Shop in Kerry Springs

To the strongest and the most stubborn woman.
I'll miss you every day, but I'm happy you're with Dad now.
Love you, Mom. Rest in peace.

CHAPTER ONE

REGINA WILLIAMS rolled over and stared up at the peeling paint on the ceiling of her bedroom and smiled.

Two weeks. That was how long she and Zack had been living in the little bungalow on Cherry Street. Even with the endless projects to do, and the sparse furnishings, they'd found joy moving into their very first home.

Of course, there were thirty years of payments ahead, even with Lori's help as co-signer and a good interest rate. That was as far as Gina would let her wealthy big sister go. She had to do this on her own. She had to prove to herself and her son they could be independent.

She had a good start, with her staging business and thrift shop and new friends and now, a wonderful place to live. Destiny, Colorado, was a great small town to raise her seven-year-old son. Zack was thriving in school and he was making friends. He was finally coming out of his shell, and maybe putting their old life where it belonged. In the past.

She climbed out of bed, slipped on her robe as she walked into the hall. She hesitated at Zack's door, then decided to put on coffee first. In the kitchen, she drew back the curtains at the French doors that overlooked the backyard.

This was the view that had sold her on the house—also the acre of land out back. Springtime in Colorado was an array of color and she had already planned out her flower garden in her head.

Right now she'd better get her busy day started. Coffee made, she walked down the hall, knocked on her son's door and opened it. "Rise and shine, kiddo." No response. Zack had always been a slow starter. She went across the hall to the bathroom and turned on the light, then the shower.

"Come on, Zack," she called. "I need to get to work and you have school." She walked back to the bunk beds, to find the top bunk empty. So she glanced under to the lower bed, but no child.

"Zack," she called, and pushed around the blankets. "Honey, we don't have time to play around. So come out of hiding."

Fear began to build as she glanced around the room. That was when she saw the curtains blowing from the open window. She rushed over to find the screen missing.

"No, God. No!" Her heart stopped then started racing as she frantically checked the closet, then under the bed, calling her son.

"Zack. Oh, God. Where are you? Please come out." Even as she pleaded, something in the back of her mind told her that her worst nightmare had come true. She returned to the bed, jerked back the blankets and found the proof. A crumpled piece of paper.

A familiar feeling of helplessness hit her. Hard. Instinctively Gina knew it was a note from her ex-husband. A shiver ran through her as she picked it up and read, *"I found you, babe. Now I got what you want. You'll be hearing from me."*

* * *

Grady Fletcher parked his truck in front of Destiny's sheriff's office and glanced up and down First Street. Mid-morning and the main street was busy with people going about their business, paying no attention to him. Just how he liked it.

He pulled up the collar of his coat and climbed out. He checked the area once again. Although he knew he was safe, old habits died hard. "Stay," he said to his trusted companion.

The German shepherd, Scout, sat in his spot in the backseat. The retired military working dog's ears perked up, waiting for his command. Grady gave a hand signal and the animal lay down. "Be right back, boy."

Grady was adjusting to his new life, too. Suddenly becoming a civilian after twenty years in the army wasn't an easy transition, especially after his last tour of duty. So temporarily living at his grandfather's old cabin was a good thing. It gave him time to heal physically and think about the future. He'd loved the solitude he found in the San Juan Mountains until he found there was a trespasser on his land.

He was going to let the sheriff handle it.

Grady walked through the front door and the room was a buzz of activity. He removed his cowboy hat and looked around. He could sense something was wrong. That was when he caught sight of the small dark-haired woman seated next to the desk. Worry was evident on her face, along with her tears. He decided his business could wait and started to leave when Reed Larkin came out of his office.

The woman stood and hurried to the sheriff. "Please, Reed, we need to start looking for Zack right now."

"And we will, Gina. First, I had to issue an Amber Alert on the boy, and find a description of Eric's last-known vehicle." He glanced over the paper. "That was a 1998 primer-gray Ford truck, Colorado license." He read off the numbers. "I have all the state agencies involved in the search, Gina."

That description sparked Grady's interest. He walked up to the twosome. "Maybe I can help."

They both turned to him, but his attention went to the pretty brunette with the wide green eyes. Grady quickly turned to the sheriff, shielding his injured side.

"Hey, Grady, I haven't seen you in town for a while."

"There's been no need, until today. You're looking for a gray truck? I might know where you can find it."

Gina forced herself to draw in her next breath as she looked up at the giant of a man. He had a head full of sandy-brown hair that curled in thick waves. His dark eyes were deep-set and edged with tiny lines. His chiseled jaw was firm and clean-shaved. She caught a glimpse of an angry red scar on the side of his neck.

Gina gasped. "Where?"

Suddenly the man turned his intense gaze on her. Her first instinct was to back away from the intimidating man, but she forced herself to listen to what he had to say.

She forced herself to move closer. "Did you see a little boy, Mr...?"

"It's Fletcher, ma'am. Grady Fletcher. There's a truck with that description on my grandfather's property. But I haven't seen anyone."

The sheriff spoke up. "This is Gina Williams, Grady. Her seven-year-old son has been taken by his father. Eric Lowell was recently released from prison for drug possession and abuse. He kidnapped the boy from his home sometime during the night. We believe he's dangerous, so any help would be appreciated. Where did you see the vehicle?"

Grady nodded. "On the northeast section of my grandfather's property," he told them. "The truck is partly hidden off the road just below Rocky Top Ridge."

Reed Larkin frowned. "Where your granddad's old mines are?"

The man nodded. "As far as I can tell the truck has been there a few days. I came in to report it. I figured they were thinking the mine is abandoned, or they're trying to jump Fletch's old claim."

"Oh, God," Gina gasped and turned to the sheriff. "Eric's been in town that long, stalking us?"

"It's okay, Gina. We're going to get him." He looked back at Grady. "When was the last time you saw the truck?"

"At dawn this morning," the man said.

Reed nodded. "Did he see you?"

"Not unless he was out walking around early. There wasn't anyone in the truck when I found it."

"Good, we have a possible location," the sheriff said. "My bet is he's holed up in one of the old mines. Can you take us there, Grady?"

He shrugged. "It's pretty rough terrain, but my dog might be able to pick up the trail. Are you and your men experienced hikers?"

Larkin nodded. "We've all had survival training. I hope the weather holds out today."

They started to walk away. Gina went after them. "Wait," she called. "Please, take me with you."

Reed went to her. "Gina, no. You can't handle the climb."

She blinked. "You have no idea what I can handle, Reed. My son is up there with a man who swore he'd get even with me. I'm not going to stand by and wait while he takes his revenge out on Zack."

The sheriff shook his head. "It's not safe."

"I can do this. And I know Eric. I know what pushes his buttons. Besides, he doesn't want Zack, or he'd be on the road heading for parts unknown."

She exchanged a glance with Grady Fletcher. "He wants me." She stood straight. "And as long as my son is safe, I'm willing to make a trade."

Minutes later, Grady stood out of the way as the sheriff made arrangements to leave. It hadn't taken long for Reed to give in to the mother's plea. Grady didn't like this plan, not one bit. Take this woman with them. No way.

He shook his head. He didn't need this problem. All he had to do was take them up to the mine, then leave the sheriff to handle the rest. Right. He wasn't made that way. In the army he'd become a take-charge-guy as a means of survival. But that was before the explosion, before he gave up his career. He shoved the memory aside and turned his thoughts to the problem at hand.

This Lowell must be a crazy bastard to come in and steal his own kid. It definitely could turn out badly.

Just then Gina Williams came out of Reed Larkin's office. She'd changed into hiking boots laced up at the bottom of her jeans. A sweatshirt under a quilted down vest would keep her warm against the cool day. She had her hair pulled back into a ponytail and a wide-brimmed hat to protect her from the elements. Springtime in Colorado was unpredictable. It could mean anything from rain to a full-blown snowstorm.

A blonde woman walked out behind the boy's mother. He recognized her as Lorelei Hutchinson Yeager. She'd pretty much owned this town since her father's death last year. Grady knew about the Hutchinsons only because of his grandfather's stories. Old Fletch had a strong dislike for any members of the town's founding family. It had something to do with disagreements over land rights.

Grady stood straighter when the two women walked his way. Ms. Williams had a stuffed toy in her hand.

"Mr. Fletcher, this is my sister, Lori Yeager. Lori, Grady Fletcher."

He nodded. "Mrs. Yeager."

She managed a smile. "It's Lori. And I can't tell you how much I appreciate your help finding my nephew. Zack means the world to us. If there's anything you need, let Reed know."

Gina looked at Grady. "The sheriff said you have a dog who can track."

He wasn't about to explain that he'd been through hell and back. "Scout was a military working dog. We're both retired now."

Gina held up a floppy-eared rabbit. "This belongs to Zack. Do you think he could pick up his scent?"

Since Scout's injury, he hadn't been put to the test. "It's worth a try."

She hugged her sister and they all walked outside. The sheriff and his two men had loaded up the white four-wheel drive SUV. After instruction to lead, Grady climbed in his own truck and Scout greeted him.

"Looks like we got some work to do. You up to it, fella?"

Surprisingly the animal let out a bark as the passenger-side door opened and the pretty Gina Williams peered in. "The other car is full. Would you mind if I rode with you?"

* * *

It seemed to take forever to get to their destination. The longest twenty minutes in Gina's life, but thanks to Grady Fletcher she now had hope of finding Zack.

She tried to calm herself as she stole a glance at the beautiful scenery along the gravel road leading to the dotting of tall pines in the distance. A stream ran alongside the winding path. She thought of Zack. Was he warm enough? Had Eric hurt him? She tensed. He'd better not have.

Suddenly she felt a nudge on her arm. She started to pull away, then discovered it was Mr. Fletcher's dog. "Hey, fella."

She looked at the man who filled up the truck cab, making Gina very aware of his presence. "Is it okay if I pet him?"

He gave her a curt nod. "It seems Scout wants the attention."

She ran her hand over the shepherd's soft, nearly black coat. "He's a beautiful dog. You said he's a military dog?"

"Yes. He served overseas until last year."

"Were you with him?"

Another curt nod.

Gina continued to rub the dog's fur. She found it gave her comfort, but nothing could stop the fear she felt for her son. She'd thought she'd been so careful. That Eric would never find them.

Out of the blue, Mr. Fletcher said, "Tell me about your…about Eric. How experienced is he with survival skills?"

"Really good. Every year, he'd go with his brothers during hunting season." She had been glad when he was away because it had meant she was safe from his abuse. "Don't put anything past him, Mr. Fletcher."

She couldn't forget the times she had, and he had made her pay. *Oh, God, Zack,* she cried silently. "Eric wasn't supposed to find us here. Destiny was our safe place." She worked to hold it together, but wasn't doing well. "We didn't tell a soul that we'd moved here. We changed our names while he was in prison." She released a sigh. "Why can't he leave us alone?"

For a long time the man didn't say anything, then added, "The sheriff will get him and he'll go back to prison."

"I pray that happens. Right now, all I'm concerned about is my son's safety."

Grady went across the stream, then drove several yards off-road, coming to a stop under a tree, next to some large boulders at the base of hillside. Before he could shut off the engine, Gina jumped out of the truck and had started up the hillside when she felt his hand on her arm.

"Hey, you just can't go running off half-cocked. At least wait for the others."

Before she could argue, a rifle shot rang out, and something hit the tree above their heads.

With a curse, Grady pushed Gina to the ground and covered her body with his. He had to get her out of there. He grabbed her close, hearing her gasp, then rolled them over and over until they were behind the tree.

Gina landed on her back and was swiftly aware of this large man. He braced his arms on either side of her head so his full weight wasn't on her. Still, she was very mindful of the fact of his powerful size. Oddly, she didn't feel panicked or threatened. She had her son to worry about.

He raised his head and those dark brooding eyes locked on hers. "You okay?"

She managed a nod. Again she caught sight of the scarred skin covering the side of his neck.

Another series of shots rang out over their heads. He moved her just as the sheriff's vehicle pulled up and parked in front of them as a shield.

Reed climbed out of the truck. His men scrambled to find cover behind large boulders. The sheriff reached them. "You two okay?"

Grady moved off the woman, trying to forget the awareness he felt. Their gaze connected for an instant before she sat up. This was trouble in more ways than he could count.

"I'm fine, but my son isn't. So I need to go up there."

She started to stand and Grady pulled her back down. "Lady, I know you aren't thinking clearly right now," he growled. "And running up there isn't going to get your son back. That maniac is holding a high-powered rife on us, and he wants you to pay."

Before Grady could stand, Gina Williams gripped his arm. "I don't care how you do it, Mr. Fletcher—just get my son out safely. Please." Tears filled those mesmerizing green eyes. "My life doesn't matter without Zack."

"We'll do whatever it takes to get the boy out of there." Grady moved away, praying he could keep his promise.

I'm so scared. Mom, help me.

Wiping away more tears, Zack sat up on the blanket and began pulling at the ropes that held his wrists and feet together. He had to get away before his dad got back. Struggling with the ropes again, he wished he were strong enough to break free. With only a little light from the lantern, he glanced around the dark cave, but couldn't see anything.

He was all alone.

He bit down on his lip, trying not to cry again. He had to get out and find his mom before Dad hurt her again.

"I got to get loose," he whispered and began to wiggle his hands back and forth feeling the burn, but continuing to fight to get out of the ropes. Using his teeth, he loosened the knot and finally his hands came out. Excited, he untied the ropes at his ankles. He stood, careful not to make any noise. He grabbed the lantern and headed toward the light in the opening. Outside he heard rifle shots so he turned and ran off in the other direction. Far away from danger.

CHAPTER TWO

GRADY stood behind the large boulder as he scanned the rocky rim with binoculars. He followed the dark figure of a man as he moved cautiously among the trees and brush. He'd seen a picture of the suspect and recognized him.

He nudged the sheriff beside him. "Lowell's up there, but I can't see any sign of the boy. Can you?"

Reed looked through his glasses, then said, "No, no sign of Zack, but that's definitely Eric Lowell. We can't rush him. The boy could get hurt. If this guy came all this way to take his son away from his ex-wife, he isn't going to give up easily."

"He'll never give up."

Grady looked over his shoulder to see that Gina approached them.

"I thought you promised to stay in the vehicle. It's not safe here."

She shook her head. "He's got Zack. My child isn't safe with him."

The panicked look on her face tore at Grady. It sent him a painful reminder of what he'd lost. Only he never deserved to have a family in the first place.

"You've got to let me go up there, Reed. Make a trade. Eric wants me. He wants to punish me. Please,

Reed," she pleaded. "Eric knows he's going back to prison. So he has nothing to lose." She wiped the tears that escaped her eyes. "I can't let him hurt Zack. I can't."

When she started to walk into the clearing, Grady grabbed her right arm as another rifle shot rang out. He pulled her back against the rock wall and shielded her. Grady had to work to get his breathing and heart rate under control. That was too close. This lunatic was playing for keeps. "Lady, you've got to stop with the crazy stunts," he growled.

She tossed him a stubborn look. "It doesn't matter. Nothing matters without my son."

"What do you think will happen to Zack if you get yourself killed? You need to let the sheriff handle this."

"Okay, but you don't understand. I can't leave my son up there." She nodded to the ridge. "I promised Zack. I promised him I wouldn't let his dad hurt us again. Please, you've got to help me."

He hated that this woman got to him. As much as Grady wanted to, it was impossible to walk away from this. He turned to Reed Larkin. "What's your next move, Sheriff?"

"I wish I had an answer. I can't take a chance that he'll harm the boy." Larkin gave him a hard look. "You know the area, Fletcher. Is there a back way in?"

Grady nodded, remembering the summers he'd tracked after old Fletch. "You can come in along Miner's Ridge. It's pretty narrow, and it'll take about fifteen minutes, but if Lowell is focused on watching for his ex-wife, we might be able to catch him by surprise. Give me a little time to scope the area."

Grady started to walk back to his truck to arm himself when Larkin stopped him. "I can't ask you to do this."

"You didn't. I volunteered."

"Then I'll need to deputize you first. Do you have a problem with that? I can't let a civilian get involved."

Grady paused as he looked at this woman still gripping that floppy-eared rabbit. Suddenly memories of his past life flashed before him, the picture of the stuffed animals that lined the shelf in his infant son's room. Toys the baby never got the chance to see or play with. He quickly shook it away. "Do what you need to do."

After the sheriff had sworn him in, Grady hurried back to his vehicle and opened the door. Immediately the shepherd stood in the backseat. Scout hesitated. The dog hadn't worked since Afghanistan when he'd been injured. Yet since they'd returned home, Grady had adopted Scout, hoping to get involved in some search-and-rescue operations. It was a good time to test him.

"Come on, boy. We've got a kid to find." The shepherd jumped out of the backseat and waited for his next command.

Grady reached back inside the vehicle, took the Glock from under the driver's seat and tucked the gun in the waistband of his jeans against his back. He was going to be prepared for anything.

Reed appeared. "I see you don't need me to issue you a weapon." The sheriff looked concerned. "I'm going to send one of my men with you."

"No. Alone. I'll move faster and with less chance of being seen." He stared at the sheriff. "You have to trust me on this."

"Okay." Reed Larkin handed him a small radio. "Here, you'll need this to communicate with us."

Grady took it, then walked over to Gina Williams, seeing the fear on her face. "I'll do everything I can to bring the boy back. So don't try anything stupid, or the sheriff will send you back to town. Let us handle this."

She nodded. "Just hurry. Please!"

Grady settled her in the truck and then he went to the sheriff. Grady knew these mountains. His grandpa had taken him around every mine and cliff along this face of the mountain range. He glanced at his dog. "Come on, boy, let's find Zack." He prayed that his words would come true. Maybe this time he would be there when someone's child needed him.

Gina watched as Grady and Scout started up the back side of the mountain. She began to pray that they would be able to get to her son before any harm came to him. She closed her eyes and could feel her ex-husband's slap across her face just as if it were happening again.

But it never stopped at just a slap. There were also those closed fists that slammed into her body. A tear dropped to her cheek and she quickly wiped it away.

No! She wasn't going to let Eric win again. She was going to make a life for her son here in Destiny. Zack was going to have a happy childhood. She wasn't going to let Eric hurt her little boy again. Even if she had to stop him herself.

"Gina."

She opened her eyes to see Reed standing next to the truck. "I wish I could tell you everything is going to be all right, but I can't. Only you know your ex. Has he ever hurt his son?"

"He hadn't until the last time. That's when Eric learned that he could inflict more pain on me by making Zack his target."

Reed's nostrils flared. "I swear, Gina, we'll do everything possible to get Zack away from him. Grady Fletcher is retired army. He's served overseas and is combat trained." The radio squawked. "That's Fletcher."

He pulled the radio out and spoke into it. "Larkin, here."

"I've reached the mine. He could be inside, or Zack could be there. Since I can't see Lowell, I don't know. You need to draw him out."

"Roger." The sheriff looked at Gina. "We need to draw Eric out in the open."

"Use me," she said, and started out of the truck. "I can distract him." She wanted Grady Fletcher to get a good shot at him.

"Give me a few minutes," the sheriff said, then signed off. "Gina, don't do anything foolish. Your ex isn't worried about leaving here. He wants revenge on you."

"I don't care. Zack is the only thing that matters."

"But he needs his mother, too."

"Just not a mother who's let him down so many times," she breathed. "But not this time, not any more."

Grady was pressed flat against the rock wall as he moved toward his target. He gave the hand signal for Scout to stay behind and continued around the boulder. There he heard the sheriff call to Lowell.

"Hey, Eric, your wife wants to talk to you."

Nothing. There was no movement, no sign of the guy. "Come on, you bastard," Grady breathed.

Then he heard Gina's voice. "Eric!" she called. "Eric, please talk to me. I know you don't want to hurt Zack. So I want to make a trade. Zack for me."

Lowell finally spoke. "I'm not falling for that," he told her.

Grady got a location. The kidnapper was just on the other side of the boulder. He looked down at Scout to see the animal's ears go up. He gave a hand signal to stay. The animal obeyed.

Again, Gina called out. "Please, Eric. I'll do whatever you want. Just don't hurt Zack. Please."

"I like to hear you beg, Gina," Lowell said. "Come on, convince me some more."

That was when Grady saw him. The man came out just enough to get into his line of sight. He looked to be around six feet tall. His body was lean and strong, probably from working out in prison. Grady wasn't impressed. Not by a man who used his strength to beat up on women. He just hoped the guy wasn't too smart.

Lowell called his ex-wife a few choice names. "Tell me what you want, wife. You always want something." The man moved toward the ledge. He knelt down for protection. "I'll need more than just you, if you want my son. That big sister of yours inherited a boatload of money. I want a cut."

"How much?" Gina asked without hesitation.

"A few million should get me where I want to go. I'll also need transportation."

There was a pause, then Gina said, "It's going to take some time."

"You got an hour," he told her.

Grady saw his chance and took it. He came out behind the guy, just as he turned around. Grady managed to knock Eric's rifle out of his hand, but that didn't stop him.

Lowell charged at him, landing several blows, then Grady got in a good one, knocking the man down. He called to Scout once he had subdued Eric on the ground in a choke hold.

"I got him," Grady yelled down to the sheriff, then to Lowell he said, "I wouldn't move if I were you." He nodded toward the growling dog. "Scout will catch you. And I haven't fed him today."

Eric cursed but didn't put up a fight as Larkin and his men showed up. One of the deputies took charge and cuffed Lowell. Larkin finished reading him his rights when Gina Williams showed up.

She ran to her ex. "Where is Zack?" she demanded.

"Go to hell," he said. His words were slurred, his eyes glassy. Drugs, in all likelihood.

Grady walked up. "Let's check the mine," he said, taking out his penlight and heading to the opening that had once been boarded up but now showed signs of some of the boards having been pulled away. He stepped through the slats, Larkin and Gina right behind him.

"Come, Scout," he called to his dog.

The shepherd immediately went into the darkness and Grady turned on the flashlight, and followed.

Gina cried out, "Zack! Mom's here and you're safe. Zack!" There wasn't a sound, then a bark from Scout. They walked carefully through the maze of rocks and mining equipment. Then they reached the wide opening. That was where they saw the light and sleeping bags and camp lanterns. There was a pile of ropes abandoned on the blanket.

Gina searched around. "Where's Zack?"

"Not sure," the sheriff said. "Maybe Eric moved him." He flashed the light around the cave and over the piles of blankets to the empty food containers. Then he picked up the knotted ropes. "Do you think Zack could have got away?" He glanced at Grady. "Is there another way out?"

Grady had to think a minute. Then he heard Scout's bark again. "This way." He started off and the others followed. They were led through a maze of rocks until they saw some light and were outside in the back of the cliff. There was no sign of the boy.

"Where is he?" Gina demanded.

Not waiting for an answer, she returned to the front of the cave. Marching over to her ex-husband, she began pounding him with her fists. "Where's Zack? Tell me. Damn you, tell me."

Lowell tried to move, but the deputies held him there. "Get her the hell away from me."

When Reed Larkin finally pulled Gina back, Grady could see her tears on her face. He was about ready to give her something to beat the SOB with.

Gina couldn't hold back any more and sobbed. "Where's my son?"

An evil grin appeared on the jerk's face. "Hell, Gina, I hid him so deep, you'll never find him."

Suddenly Grady reached out and gripped Eric's shirt, getting the man's attention. "You'd better hope that's a lie, because if anything you said has one ounce of truth in it, I'll personally take care of you myself. So I suggest you don't push any more of my buttons, or I'll bury you so deep no one will find you," he said through clenched teeth, then he finally released Lowell, causing him to stumble backward.

"Hey, he threatened me," Eric cried.

"I didn't hear anything," the sheriff told him, and the deputies agreed. "Maybe you better talk, and fast."

"Who the hell are you?"

Fletcher moved closer. "Your worst nightmare. I've done two tours of duty in Afghanistan. I know a lot of ways to torture someone, and get rid of the body."

Lowell's eyes grew wide. "I swear, I left Zack back

in the cave and he was tied up when I came out. I don't know where he is now."

Grady got in his face again. "I'd better not find out you're lyin'."

Eric cringed, looking like the coward he was. "Sheriff, get him away from me, I told you everything I know."

"Take him down to the truck," Reed said.

After the deputies took Lowell off to the vehicle, Gina turned to the sheriff. "We've got to go look for Zack."

"We will, Gina," Reed promised, and turned to Grady. "Could Scout find the boy?"

"We can try." Grady looked around the dark area, but Scout wasn't there. He put two fingers in his mouth and whistled. "Scout. Come." There wasn't even the sound of a bark. Now it was time for Grady to panic.

"Please, don't hurt me," Zack cried as the big wolf came toward him. He raised his shaking hand and waved, hoping the animal would leave his hiding place. "Just go away. Please."

Zack took off running. He wasn't sure what he was more afraid of, the animal or his dad finding him. He climbed the rough hillside, and went through a group of trees, but every time he looked back the big wolf was still following him. He tripped on a rock and cried out as he fell. He rolled over and saw his bloody palms. It hurt so bad, but he wasn't going to cry. He just had to get away.

He got up and started to walk again, hoping he could find someone who would get him back to his mom. He looked up at the sky. It was getting late and it was going to be dark soon. That scared him. Nighttime was when bad things happened. He glanced over his shoulder to see the wolf was still following him. Zack climbed over the next rock and stopped. There was a coyote, then soon there were three of them.

Suddenly the wolf following him took off after the wild dogs. The animals fought, and soon the coyotes ran away, but not the wolf, who came back to him. Afraid, Zack backed away, but the animal still came closer. Then he saw a collar and a tag hanging from his neck. "You're a dog?"

As if he understood, the animal barked at him.

All at once the wind began to blow and Zack hugged himself. It began to rain, and lightning and thunder weren't far behind.

The dog barked again and started off, but stopped and waited for him. Maybe the dog was taking him home. Zack went after him, but they came to another mine and the dog slipped inside, showing him the way.

Shivering, he went inside the dark old mine. He didn't know what else to do. Inside, he stayed close to the opening, and the fading light, but couldn't help but be curious by all the treasures. An old mining car sat on tracks. He wished there were some blankets to keep him warm. It began to pour rain outside and he stepped back. The dog came up beside him, and Zack stood very still, then he reached down and petted him. His fur was soft.

"Good dog," Zack managed to say.

The animal nudged him away from the entrance and Zack sat. The dog sat, too. "Can I see your collar?" Zack carefully reached for the silver tag and read the letters.

"U.S. Army. Your name is Scout. Wow, you're an army dog. You can protect me."

Scout laid his head on Zack's leg, and he was beginning to feel a little better. Now, if only his mom would find him.

CHAPTER THREE

THREE hours later, and exhausted from the search, everyone stood next to the sheriff's vehicles to figure out the next move. They'd had to wait out the heavy rain, then had gone back out and combed the area once it let up, but any trail of her son had been washed out.

"But we can't leave Zack out there," Gina cried.

A frustrated Reed Larkin said, "Of course not, Gina, but it's getting dark. I need to go back to town and get more volunteers and we'll start out again at first light. The men need to eat, and get some rest."

"It could be too late by then," Gina argued.

The sheriff turned to Grady Fletcher. "Is there a chance your dog might be with Zack?"

Gina was hopeful. "Is that true?"

Grady nodded. "Scout might have got the boy's scent and gone after him. If the dog couldn't get the boy to follow him back to us, he'd stay."

She was hopeful. "So Zack's not alone out there?"

"It's a possibility," Grady told her. "I don't know for sure." He hesitated. "Scout had some injuries while in Afghanistan."

Gina frowned. "Injuries? So you don't know how he'll act? Could he harm Zack?"

Grady shook his head. "Scout wouldn't hurt anyone

unless he's given provocation. If he found your son, he's been trained to stay with him. He'll protect him with his life."

The sheriff stepped in. "I know I can't get you to go back to town, Gina, but I can call Lori."

"No, I don't want her out in this weather. She's pregnant and Jace is out of town."

"So you're going to spend the night in a truck?" the sheriff argued. "And there's more rain expected."

"I'll be all right." She turned to Grady. "That is, if you'd be willing stay, too. Of course I'll pay you for your time."

The man straightened. "I don't want your money. I'll stay for the boy and for my dog. But a better plan might be to go to my grandfather's cabin up the road. At least dry off and get something to eat."

Reed Larkin stepped in. "That's a good idea, Gina. You can't just keep wandering around these mountains. You'll get lost. That isn't going to help Zack."

How could she leave her son? "How far away is the cabin?"

"About a half mile from here," he offered. "You'll at least be close by, and if Scout leads the boy out, he'll bring him to the cabin."

She looked back at Reed. "Go, Gina," he told her. "You're chilled to the bone. I'll be back at first light."

It had been a long time since she'd trusted a man, outside of her new brother-in-law, Jace, and a few of the townspeople. It looked like she didn't have much of a choice.

"Thank you, Grady," Gina said. "I promise I won't be a problem."

Grady knew that wasn't true. Gina Williams had already caused him the kind of trouble he didn't need right now. "I know. And you'll at least dry off and get some food in you."

The sheriff stopped Grady. "I'll be back at dawn." He handed him his card. "If anything happens before then call my cell phone."

Then the men loaded into the vehicles and drove down the road.

"Come on, let's get you warmed up." Grady helped Gina into the truck, then turned on the heater, trying to stop her shivering. The temperature had already dropped with the fading daylight, and with the combination of the rain, it was damn cold. He, too, was worried about the boy, praying he had found cover.

He drove along the bumpy road that led to the old log cabin that he'd called home for the past three months. In the dim light, the place didn't look much better than when he'd officially moved in a few months ago, knowing his grandfather needed a lot of help for his recovery.

After parking the truck, he got out to help his guest, but she'd already jumped down by the time he reached her. He climbed the steps to the porch that sorely needed to be replaced. It was one of the many things on his list. He would get to that in time. But it meant he wasn't exactly ready to have guests.

He unlocked the door and swung it open and allowed Gina to step inside. He followed and quickly went to the back room and switched on the compressor, then returned and turned on the table lamp.

"Oh, my," she said. "It really is rustic."

He glanced at her. "There's a generator for the refrigerator and lights, but wait until you need to use the facilities. They're still out back."

She shrugged. "Then maybe I should head there now."

With a nod, he showed her the little house toward the back of the cabin. He waited on the porch as the last of day turned into night. It only took a few minutes before she came hurrying back to the cabin.

Inside again he watched her examine her surroundings in the main room. A huge stone fireplace and rough log walls were as far as the rustic charm went. It got worse with the old sofas and two chairs that were covered in a faded fabric. A big scarred table took up most of the kitchen area. He'd like to get rid of a lot of it.

Old Fletch had had the entire space crowded with furniture. His grandfather never threw out anything. Thank goodness he hadn't inherited that trait from the old man. Since he'd heard about his grandfather's accident, he'd been doing double duty. Once he'd arrived here from Texas, he'd been going to the nursing home to oversee Fletch's recovery from his broken hip. He'd also been trying to clean up this place by hauling things off to the dump.

He handed her a blanket and lit the logs in the fireplace. "It'll be warm soon."

"I'm fine, really," she said, unable to stop her shivering. "I can't tell you how much I appreciate you letting me stay here. I just need to be close by."

"I understand." He went into the kitchen area. "I'm going to reheat some stew I made last night."

"Please don't feel you have to wait on me." She stood by the fire. "I'll probably just sit right here."

"I'm going to eat, so you might as well."

She nodded. "Okay, what can I do to help?"

He nodded toward the cupboard as she came into the kitchen area. "The bowls and spoons are in there."

Gina did as he asked. She was surprised at the cabin, especially the array of furniture crammed inside. The cabinet that held the dishes was an antique. "You have a lot of…things."

"It all belongs to my grandfather. He's been in a nursing home. I've been trying to clear out most of this stuff since I came here a few months ago."

She looked at him. "Are you selling the furniture? I might know of someone who's interested."

"In this junk?"

She raised an eyebrow. "Your grandfather has some nice pieces. This cabinet is probably an antique. It's a Hoosier." She glanced over the scarred wood. "It might need work, but it's worth some money."

He turned up the flame on the camp stove and set the pan on top. "Really?"

Gina once again saw on his neck the long burn scar that ran past his collar. She didn't want to stare, but it was hard not to. "You said Scout was injured by a bomb. Were you with him?"

He stopped, but didn't answer for a while. Then he looked at her with those dark brooding eyes. "Are you asking if that's where I got my scar?"

She nodded.

"Yeah. It's not pretty, but I was one of the lucky ones."

Grady tried not to think about that day, or the two men he'd lost.

"I'm sorry. It must have been horrible."

"Yeah, war usually is."

Grady thought back to the two young soldiers, Jimmy and Vince. After he'd been well enough to leave the hospital, Grady had made a trip to West Virginia to visit Jimmy Prescott's family, then he'd gone on to Georgia to see Vince Johnson's kin.

Gina drew his attention back to the present. "What about you?" she asked. "Do you have any family?"

He didn't like where this was headed. "You sure are full of questions."

She shrugged. "Seems you know everything about me and my sordid past."

He frowned. "It's not sordid. You did nothing wrong. The man beat you. There's nothing lower than that. You did the right thing by sending him to jail."

"Not as soon as I should have," she admitted. "I had the misconception that I could love Eric enough to make him stop." She raised her chin. "He just didn't love me enough to want to. Now, my son is paying for it."

He stopped himself from going to her. She didn't need the kind of comfort he was willing to give. "Hey, we all have regrets," he told her. Hell, he had a boatload of them. "Sometimes love isn't enough." Removing the pan from the stove, he carried it to the table and emptied the stew into the bowls. "Sit down. You need to eat."

She did as he asked. "I'm really not hungry."

He sat across from her. "Eat anyway. You need strength to hike around the mountains. I don't need to have to carry you out of there tomorrow."

She took a small bite and chewed slowly. "You're good at giving orders."

He swallowed a spoonful of stew. "I've had a lot of years to practice."

Those deep green eyes widened and he felt a stirring of awareness. "How long were you in the army?"

He watched her take another bite. "I went in the day I turned eighteen, and got discharged last December. Twenty years." When had he suddenly become such an open book?

"You don't look old enough."

And she looked far too young for him to think about anything beyond helping to find her son. So he needed to stop the direction of his thoughts. "Spoken like a respectful youngster."

She raised an eyebrow. "I'm not so young."

"What, twenty-five?"

"Twenty-seven…my next birthday."

Still far too young for him. Think of her as a kid sister. That didn't work, either. He was drawn to her intriguing eyes once again, then his gaze lowered to her mouth and he felt the reaction like a slam in the gut. He glanced away. It had been nearly two years since he'd reacted so strongly to a woman. Not since his marriage had fallen apart. Definitely not since the accident. He stood. "Do you want any more?"

"No thank you. I'm finished."

"Okay, if you need to use the bathroom again, I suggest you go now." He looked out the window. "It's started to rain again."

She nodded. "I'm fine."

Well, he wasn't. So the sooner they found the boy the better. Then he could get back to his life.

"You think you can get away from me? Think again, bitch."

Gina huddled in the corner, trying to protect her body from Eric's vicious blows. "Please stop!" she cried, praying he'd tire and let her alone.

"Never. I'll always find you. You'll never get away. Never." He stepped back, stumbling drunkenly.

Zack suddenly appeared. "Stop hurting my mom," he cried, and began hitting his dad. "Go away. Leave us alone."

Eric grabbed the boy, swung back his fist and she screamed. "No! Don't hit him! No!"

"Gina! Wake up"

She felt someone shaking her. She finally opened her eyes and saw the large figure leaning over her. She gasped and pushed him away. "Please, don't," she cried and scurried to the end of the sofa.

Grady stepped back and raised his hands in surrender. "Hey, it's me, Grady. You had a bad dream. I woke you, that's all. I'm not going to hurt you, Gina. You're safe here."

Gina brushed her hair back, trying to slow her breathing. "Oh, God, Grady, I'm so sorry." She glanced up to see the man standing there in the dark shadows in a pair of Levi's and a T-shirt over a well-toned body. "Please tell me I didn't hit you. Are you all right?"

In the shadowed light, Grady stared back at her, knowing it best to keep his distance. He wished he could get his hands on Lowell again. "Question is, are you?"

She nodded, but avoided any eye contact. "The nightmare must have been triggered by Eric taking Zack."

At least she'd got a few hours of sleep. He'd covered her with a blanket before going into the one bedroom in the cabin.

She finally looked at him. "Is it light enough to start searching again?"

He nodded. "I expect by the time we have some coffee, it'll be daylight." He sure wasn't going to get any more sleep.

After Grady dressed in fresh jeans and a shirt, he made coffee and they pulled on their coats and headed to the truck. It only took a few minutes to get back to the original spot where Eric's truck had been parked the day before. Where Gina Williams's nightmare had started.

Grady ended the call to the sheriff and put his cell phone back into his pocket. "Larkin said they'll be here in ten minutes."

"I can't wait." Gina opened the truck door. "I'm going to head up." She was out of the cab.

Grady jumped out and went after her. He grabbed her by the arm, and she immediately jerked away. He raised his hands in surrender.

"Sorry. I just don't want you to run off. You don't know the area and could get lost, too. Besides, I want to check out another mine, the Lucky Penny." He pointed to a different direction. "We didn't get to it last night."

"Why not?"

They started climbing the slope. "For one thing, it was too dark and it's a lot farther."

"Why do you think Zack could be there?"

"Scout knows the mines around here. I've been working with him there on some search-and-rescue training."

Gina was frustrated. Her son had been out in the elements all night and all she wanted was to find him. "Okay, let's go there."

He nodded and they started their hike to the Lucky Penny.

She managed to keep up with him. "Do you think Zack would follow your dog to safety?"

"Your son seems pretty resourceful. He was smart enough to get untied and run away from his dad, then he's smart enough to stay out of the weather."

"But he doesn't know that he's safe from his dad. He might still be hiding."

Zack was shivering when he woke up. He'd been cold all night, even with Scout sleeping beside him, keeping him warm. He was still next to him now. He wished it were his mom with him. He was so scared and his scraped hand hurt.

"What do we do, Scout? I don't want my dad to find me. He's mean, and he hurts Mom." He stroked the dog's fur. "He'll hurt me, too, because I ran away." He brushed away a tear, hating to cry.

The dog got up and gave a bark.

Maybe Scout could protect him. But his dad had a gun. He wiped away more tears. "Why can't my dad just leave us alone?" he said, making a fist. "I don't want to go away and have to hide again. I like living in Destiny with my mom, Aunt Lori and Uncle Jace and my cousin Cassie."

The dog cocked his head as if he were listening to every word.

"We have a new house and I'm gonna try out for baseball next month. I get to have a birthday party this year." He didn't care about that. He only wanted his mom.

The animal made a whining sound and looked toward the cave opening.

Zack was suddenly afraid again. What if his dad got his mom, and hurt her? He didn't know what to do.

Suddenly the animal jumped up and went to the opening, then he looked back and barked. He came back several times, and nudged at him before he ran outside.

"Wait, Scout," Zack cried and took off after him. Once he was outside, the sunlight nearly blinded him. The dog barked again, then he heard a voice calling his name.

He tried not to cry, but he couldn't help it. "Mom!" he yelled, and followed Scout. "Mom!"

* * *

Gina stopped when she heard the sound. She grabbed Grady's arm. "I hear something."

Grady paused and the next sound was that of a dog barking. He put two fingers in his mouth and let loose with a loud whistle. He was rewarded with another bark.

"This way," he said. "It's coming from the Lucky Penny." He pointed toward their left, then took her hand and helped her climb up the slope. When they reached the cluster of boulders, a dog and child appeared.

Her heart was beating wildly. "Zack," she cried, and ran to her son.

"Mom," he cried, throwing himself into her arms.

"Oh, Zack." The tears poured out of her as she hugged him tight, breathing in his familiar smell. Even with the mixture of dirt and sweat, it was heavenly. "Oh, thank goodness you're safe." She pulled back and did a quick examination. "We were so worried. Where did you go?"

The child looked worried. "When I got untied, I was afraid Dad would come back to get me. So I ran away. Where is he?"

"Oh, honey." She smiled. "Don't worry. Sheriff Larkin has your dad in jail. Mr. Fletcher helped capture him." She hugged her son again. "He's never going to hurt us again. I promise, Zack. I promise. You must have been so scared."

Her son pulled away. "I was at first." He glanced down at the dog. "Scout came and stayed with me." His brown eyes widened. "Mom, he's a military dog."

She managed a nod. "I know. He's trained to find people and I'm so grateful that he found you."

"He kept me warm all night long." Zack looked at Grady. "Is he your dog?"

"Yes, he is." Grady stood next to the animal, who sat

perfectly still. "We've been in a lot of tight situations together. Scout was trained to find bombs. I guess now he can add little boys to the list."

Gina had completely forgotten about the introductions. "Zack, this is Mr. Fletcher. He's helped me search for you."

"Thank you. I'm glad you had Scout." Zack went over to the animal. "Can I pet him?"

"I know Scout would like that."

Grady watched the affection between the two. This was a new experience for Scout. A child was hard to resist, could even be distracting. Grady glanced at Gina Williams. So was his mother.

"Maybe we should head back down," he said. "You need to get warm and checked out to make sure you're okay."

They started walking down the slope just as the sheriff's vehicle appeared next to his truck. The next ten minutes were chaotic as Grady stood back and let the paramedic look over the boy. Then they all piled into the vehicle.

"I can't thank you enough for all you did, Grady." She smiled for real this time and he found he liked it too much. "My son is everything to me," she managed to say.

"Then you'd better go tend to him." Scout sent a bark toward his new friend in the SUV. Grady watched Gina get into the vehicle and drive off. Suddenly he was alone once again, and realized it wasn't what he truly wanted at all.

Be careful what you wish for.

CHAPTER FOUR

FOUR hours later Gina stood at her sister, Lori's, family room entrance and watched her son sleeping on the pull-out sofa bed. She still felt shaky, thinking about the thirty-six-hour ordeal. Worse, how things could have turned out.

A tear fell against her cheek. Zack was back safe with her. She had so many people to thank; one in particular, Grady Fletcher. The stranger who had put everything else aside and led the sheriff to Eric, then had stayed with her the entire time, keeping her sane until they found Zack. And Scout. What a special dog to protect her son.

"Is he asleep?" Lori whispered as she came up behind her.

Gina nodded, and followed her sister into the kitchen. "I promised I'd stay close by."

Lori motioned for her to take a seat at the large kitchen island. "I think we're close enough to hear him if he wakes."

Technically her half sister, Lorelei Hutchinson Yeager was a pretty blonde with big brown eyes and a generous heart. Last fall she'd come to Destiny when she inherited her estranged father's fortune. She'd fallen in love and married a building contractor, Jace Yeager, and moved into his house with his daughter, Cassie. Just recently they'd got a big surprise when Lori learned she was pregnant.

Gina glanced around the newly remodeled room. Jace had done a great job of refinishing the fixer-upper home, especially the kitchen. The large space had custom maple cabinets, granite counters and top-of-the-line stainless-steel appliances.

Gina was proud she'd helped Lori add some special touches with the burnt-orange paint and bright yellow accents.

Lori set a cup of hot tea in front of her. "Here, drink this."

"Thanks," Gina told her. "You should sit down, too. You have to be tired."

"I'm fine. Really."

When Gina was growing up, Lori had been more than a big sister. She had filled in where their mother couldn't or wouldn't. Still Gina had become a rebellious teenager when she'd met wild boy Eric Lowell. Lori had never deserted her though, especially when things had got rough and Eric had begun knocking her around.

Last fall when Lori had come to Destiny to claim her inheritance from her father, Lyle Hutchinson, she'd sent for Gina and Zack, hoping they all could start a new life here together. Then somehow Eric had found them.

Gina felt the emotions churning up again, but this time she couldn't push them away and she began to sob.

Lori shot around the island and pulled her sister into her arms. "Oh, honey. Let it out. You've been through hell the past two days."

Gina cried until her throat was raw and she finally wiped away the last of her tears. "I thought we were safe. How foolish could I be to think Eric would leave us alone?"

"Well, he's going to be staying away now. He'll be in jail. If the kidnapping charge doesn't stick, shooting at the sheriff and at you should carry some weight."

Heavens, she prayed that would work. "He's got off before."

"This is his third offence, Gina. That hateful man took my nephew and he isn't going to get away with that. Not this time."

Gina thought back to all the people who'd helped her in the past few days. The entire town had volunteered. They'd cooked meals, asked to be deputized and searched for Zack, or just prayed for his safe return. Once again she thought of the one man who had truly helped her find her son.

"Lori, what do you know about Grady Fletcher?"

Her sister blinked at her question, then smiled. "Not much, only that he's been in the bank a few times. I know more about his grandfather, Joe Fletcher. The old miner is recuperating from a broken hip at Shady Haven Nursing Home. Since Grady was listed as next of kin, he's been handling things until Fletch gets back on his feet. I'm not sure that's going to happen since his grandfather has to be in his eighties."

"So he doesn't live here?"

Lori shrugged. "It would be nice if he did. From what Reed told me about what happened on the mountain, I'd say Grady is a take-charge kind of guy. And for what he did for Zack, he's pretty high on my list of good people. Not bad-looking, either."

Gina wasn't surprised by her sister's assessment. She hadn't had much time to notice, but once the dust had settled, she had taken a look at the handsome man. "You'd better not let Jace hear you talk like that."

Lori smiled. "He has nothing to worry about. I only have eyes for my husband."

"That's good to know."

They turned around to see Jace Yeager standing in the doorway. The tall, dark and handsome man was smiling at his wife. "Because I'm kind of crazy about you, too."

Lori rushed across the room, wrapped her arms around him and rewarded him with a tender kiss. "I thought you weren't coming home until tomorrow," she said.

"My family needed me. So I made it happen." He walked over to Gina and pulled her into a big hug. "I'm so sorry I wasn't here for you and Zack."

She nodded. "It's okay, Jace. We got him back and that's all that matters."

That was when they heard a child's cry from the other room. Gina jumped up and hurried to the sofa bed.

"It's okay, honey." She sat on the edge of the bed and pulled her son into her arms.

There were tears in her son's eyes. "Mom, I dreamed Dad was coming after me."

"Never. He's never going to get near you ever again." She looked up at Lori and Jace. "Hey, Uncle Jace came home so he could be with you."

Jace walked to the sofa. "That's right, partner. I heard you had a rough few days."

The child nodded eagerly. "Yeah, I got tied up in a cave."

Gina saw her brother-in-law stiffen, working to control his anger. He kept his voice calm. "Man, that's bad. I'm proud of you for being smart enough to handle it."

He messed the boy's hair. "So you spent the night in a cave."

The boy's eyes grew wide. "Yeah, but Scout was with me. He's a big German shepherd. I didn't get scared too much because he was there to protect me from other animals and bad people."

"Sounds like Scout is a pretty neat dog."

Again the child nodded. "He was in the military. He's a hero like Grady." Zack looked at his mom. "I wish I had a dog like Scout. I wouldn't be afraid then."

All eyes turned to Gina. "Yeah, Mom," Jace mimicked. "A dog would be good protection."

Gina had always planned to get her son a dog once they were settled. Her house had a fenced-in yard. "I guess a dog wouldn't be a bad idea."

Her son nearly jumped into her arms. "You're the best mom in the whole world."

Those words were enough to completely sell her on the idea, and to remind her how close she'd come to losing her son. "And you're the best son in the whole world."

The next morning was Saturday, and as Gina promised, she drove her son out to the cabin to thank Grady. Even for her small all-wheel-drive vehicle, it was slow going over the pitted dirt road. She wasn't sure that she was headed in the right direction until she came through a grove of trees and finally saw the cabin in the clearing.

"Oh, boy." It wasn't much of a clearing. More like a junkyard. Something she hadn't noticed when she was here before. Suddenly she was rethinking her decision to come, wondering if Grady Fletcher just wanted to be left alone.

"Grady might be busy, Zack. I'm not sure if we should just drop in on him."

"Come on, Mom. We don't have to stay long. I want to give Scout my present."

They'd spent all morning shopping for a reward for the dog. "Okay, but if he doesn't have the time, then we leave. Mr. Fletcher is a busy man."

Then the cabin door opened and the German shepherd came out and greeted them with a bark, but stayed on the porch. Gina's heart skipped a beat when the tall man stepped through the door. He was dressed in jeans and a dark thermal shirt, showing off his muscular build. Her body reacted, not in fear but in awareness. Well, darn.

"Scout!" her son called and jumped out of the car. Zack took off running to the dog before she could stop him.

Grady stood rooted on the porch, surprised to see Gina Williams again. Then she stepped out of her car and he found his heart suddenly beating faster. He wasn't happy about that, or about the lack of sleep he'd had since the night she'd invaded his cabin.

Dressed in jeans tucked into boots and a sweater and thermal vest, she reached into the backseat and took out a cellophane-wrapped basket.

She walked toward the steps. "I hope we're not disturbing you."

She didn't want to know the answer to that. "I can take a break." He looked down at Zack. He was glad that the boy looked to be doing well. "Hey, Zack. How are you feeling today?"

He stood on the bottom step, and Scout sat eagerly on the porch waiting for a command to go greet his new friend.

"I had a nightmare last night, but then I pretended that Scout was with me and felt better." The boy waited. "Mom said I need to ask you first if I can pet Scout 'cause he might be in training." Both kid and dog looked up at him waiting for an answer.

"When he's not working he can play. And he's not working now."

Zack grinned. "I got Scout a present. Mom got you something, too." He pulled a long tug rope with a handle on the end from the bag he was carrying. "Is this okay?"

It was okay for Scout, but he didn't want anyone bringing *him* presents. Especially a distracting woman with a little boy. "Yeah, it's okay, but Scout can pull pretty hard."

"I know he's really strong."

Grady pointed to a cleared spot. "Go over in the yard."

The bright sunlight seemed to highlight all the junk that littered the area. Two rusted-out vehicles, a mess of mining equipment. "I've been trying to clear away most of this stuff, but couldn't do much until the snow melted."

Gina nodded. "I'm sure you can get a lot for the scrap metal."

"I might have hell to pay from my grandfather, but I've got someone coming here in a few days. I'm hoping it will all be cleared out." He sighed. "Then I plan to cart some stuff out of the inside so I have room to move around." He shook his head. "I don't know how the man didn't kill himself. What am I saying? He broke his hip."

The boy called Scout and they ran off to the yard. That meant he was left alone to deal with the mother.

Gina carried the basket up the steps. "I wanted to talk to you about that."

"About what?"

"Your furniture. Well, your grandfather's that is." She stepped onto the porch. "I have a thrift store in town called Second Best. If there are things you want to get rid of, I can sell them for you on consignment…."

That surprised the hell out of him. "That's what you do for a living?"

She nodded. "I kind of fell into it. I started by staging my sister's business complex, then she asked me to decorate some bank-owned properties. I got the idea for a store when I ended up with all this furniture people left behind." She nodded toward the cabin. "Seems like you have extra furniture, too. If you want to get rid of some things, I'd be happy to have a look."

"I'll check with Fletch when I visit him the next time."

"Good." She held out the package in her hands. "I also brought you a little something."

Though embarrassed by her gesture, Grady couldn't refuse her gift. "You didn't have to."

"It's not much. Really. Just some turkey and ham and cheeses from the sandwich shop in town. We wanted to thank you for everything you did. Especially having to put up with me."

Spending time with her hadn't been a burden. Finding her son had been the good part. "Hey, I was in the military for years, so I'm used to taking orders."

She made a face, but it didn't take away from her beauty. He doubted anything could. "Was I that bad?"

"You were just willing to do whatever it took to get your child back. I'm glad everything came out okay." He motioned her toward the door. "Please come in."

First, Gina glanced at Zack to see he was okay with

Scout then turned and told Grady, "He makes a great babysitter."

"Scout hasn't been around kids much, but I can see that I don't have anything to worry about. And since I've adopted him and am training him for search and rescue, I was impressed with how well he did finding Zack."

"Will you be staying here after your grandfather comes home?"

"My plans are to go back to Texas, San Antonio, outside Lackland AFB. That's where I plan to do my training with my partner."

"I see." Gina wasn't sure of what else to say as she crossed the threshold so she concentrated on her surroundings. In the daylight, she was able to get a better look. There was some junk, but she'd been right the night she stayed here. There were several good pieces, too. "Do you know what you'd like to keep?"

When she heard his sigh, she realized how close he was standing to her. "About half this," he told her. "I can barely move around as it is. "I'm going to throw out two of the sofas."

She set the basket down on the table. "Which two?"

He pointed out the two worst of the three. "I'll take them," she told him.

"You're kidding?"

"No. They're older, but the frames look to be in great shape. I can reupholster them and sell them in the shop."

"They're yours," he assured her.

Gina examined all the different antique pieces that interested her. He told her no when she asked about the Hoosier cabinet. She'd expected that, but she got a nice sideboard and two end tables to sell on consignment. And he just gave her the old rocking chair.

"Is there more?"

He arched a brow, and she caught a gleam in those dark brown eyes. Then a smile tugged at the corner of his mouth and there was a strange feeling in her stomach.

"Show me?" Her voice was a little throaty.

He didn't say a word as he walked to the doorway leading to another room. She followed tentatively as he opened the door and she stepped through into the next room.

She immediately saw the huge bed that took up most of the limited space. She got closer to the metal frame to see that it was brass, heavily tarnished, but definitely brass. "Oh, my. This is quite something."

"Oh, yeah, it is," Grady agreed. "And my grandfather was very proud of this bed."

"I take it he had it for years."

He nodded. "Ever since I can remember. And I spent a lot of summers here as a kid. Fletch was so proud that he bought it with one of his first gold strikes."

Gina walked around to the other side. "Of course he wouldn't want to sell it?"

He shrugged. "It does take up a lot of room, but probably not."

She glanced around. Like the other space the room was crowded with furniture. "There would be more room to move around if you removed one of these armoires." She went to one cabinet and examined the hand-carved detail on the doors. "This is a lovely piece. I'm not an expert, but I could have an appraiser look at it."

He hesitated, so Gina moved on to the other cabinet. "This one is nice, too. Not as well made, but I could sell it for you if you want."

This was the last thing Grady thought he'd be doing today. When Gina Williams showed up on his doorstep, he didn't think they'd end up in his bedroom. *Whoa, don't go there.*

"Grady?"

He shook off the thoughts. "Sure, I'll check with my grandfather and get back to you. Just leave me the bed and something to put clothes in. Right now my focus is working on the outside."

"Well, I should let you get back to it. I'll go."

She turned to leave and Grady reached for her arm. Then hearing her gasp, realized his mistake. He also saw the panicked look in her eyes and released her. "Sorry. I didn't mean to startle you."

"It's okay. I'm still a little jumpy."

"No, I had no right to grab you like that. Look, you don't have to leave. It's just my frustration with all this stuff in the cabin. Hell, I don't know what to do with fifty years of junk around here. I wouldn't know an antique if it bit me."

"Are you trying to get ready to sell this place?"

He shook his head. "No, but my grandfather can't continue to live like this if he wants to come back here. I'm training dogs, and since I'm staying here longer than planned, I need to build temporary kennels.

"First, I need to clear an area outside. A guy is coming Monday to haul off all the things in the front yard. So the inside of the cabin isn't a top priority."

She smiled. "You're going to train more dogs for a living."

He wanted to make a living at something he enjoyed, and that was working with dogs. "Since I'm retired from the army, I need to do something. Of course, Grandpa

Fletch could be a handful." He couldn't abandon the old man who had always been there for him.

"Sounds like a interesting man."

"He has his moments. I'll ask him about the furniture the next visit, because I can't concentrate on the cabin until then." This bedroom was getting smaller by the minute. Her scent drifted in his direction, reminding him of the things he'd lost, that he'd chosen to walk away from.

She followed him back into the main room. "Then we're out of your hair."

She headed for the door, then paused and turned back to him with those sparkling green eyes. "I have an idea. How about if when you get the okay from your grandfather, I'll handle organizing the inside of the cabin for you?" She walked back to him so he got the full effect of her beauty. Her flawless skin and perfect mouth. All that thick brown hair brushing her shoulders made his hands itch to touch it.

"There's no need for you to do that."

"I know, but you rescued my son. There's no way I can repay you for that. Please, let me help you."

He'd pretty much been a loner since his marriage had ended. His choice. And this woman wasn't helping his solitude. "Do you have someone to help you cart off this stuff?"

She nodded. "There's a man who works for my brother-in-law. He does pickups and deliveries for me, too."

He sighed. "Okay, let me check with Fletch and I'll get back to you."

Just then Zack came rushing inside. "Boy, Grady, your dog is really smart."

Grady wasn't used to having kids around. "He's been well trained."

"By you?"

"No, I'm not his first handler. A soldier named Vince Richards worked with him while in Afghanistan."

"Why do you have him?"

Grady shot a glance at Gina, then said, "Because Scout is retired and I adopted him. I've also adopted two more military dogs. They should arrive next week."

The boy's eyes widened. "Wow. I wish I could have a dog like Scout. Mom said I could get a puppy."

Grady arched an eyebrow. "A dog is a lot of responsibility and work."

The boy nodded. "I know. Mom said I have to feed him and take him for walks."

And Gina added, "And make sure he doesn't have accidents in the house."

"And I want him to protect me, too." Zack turned to Grady. "Can you help me teach a dog to do that?"

Grady hesitated, knowing the boy was still traumatized over what had happened. "I'll see what I can do."

CHAPTER FIVE

GRADY drove his truck through the gates of Shady Haven Nursing Home. With the brick and red-cedar shingles, the two-story building looked like a mountain resort. That was only part of the facility, too. There was also a drug rehab center on the far side of the property. And they'd added a newer section, the senior assisted-living apartments.

He walked through the double doors and the inside was just about as impressive. A large reception area had a fireplace and gleaming hardwood floors. In an adjoining room, Grady could see several patients in wheelchairs. One of them was old Joe Fletcher.

He walked in past residents playing games at different tables. His grandfather was playing cards, no doubt taking their money, too.

"Hey, Fletch, what are you up to?"

The thin man with the leathered skin glanced in his direction. "Hey, Grady." He smiled. "Good to see you. Hey, everyone, this is my grandson. Master Sergeant Grady Fletcher."

He pulled up a chair, swung it around and straddled it. "Come on, Joe, I'm retired now. It's just Grady."

"But you're a hero." Those same dark eyes looked back at him. "I heard about the boy."

Grady was surprised. "That was an accident. I found someone trespassing on your land. I told the sheriff."

The old man gave him a toothy grin. "I'm proud, son. Now, can you break me out of here?"

"Whoa, you aren't even healed yet. You need physical therapy." He leaned forward. "And about coming home. It's a death trap there."

Those bony shoulders lifted in a shrug. "So I've collected a few things."

Grady arched an eyebrow. "A few! I'd say, in certain circles you could be known as a hoarder." He sobered. "I need to get rid of a few things so you can get a walker around the place."

The old man grumbled some, then said, "Whatever you think is best, son. Just leave my bed alone."

It was a few days before Gina heard from Grady when he gave her the okay to come out. It took another day before she could get Mac Burleson and his brother, Connor, to drive up to the Fletcher place. They both had other jobs, working for her brother-in-law at Yeager Construction. She couldn't pay them the same money as Jace and she didn't need them too often.

She was reluctant to come along, not knowing if Grady really wanted her there. She also wondered if it was his burn scars that kept him out of town and on the mountain. Somehow, she thought he might just be a solitary man by nature. No sign of a wedding band. Of course, that didn't mean there wasn't someone special. Maybe he was at a loose end since he retired from the army and had to stay here until his grandfather got better.

She shook away any personal thoughts of Mr. Fletcher. It was none of her business. She was interested only in his furniture, not him. She pulled her car up next to the familiar truck, leaving room for Mac's vehicle. She climbed out and that was when she noticed the changes.

The rusted old cars that littered the yard were gone, along with the mining equipment. The grass had even been mowed. Along with the Burlesons, she went up the walk and saw the new wooden steps to the porch. The door opened and Grady came out.

"Good morning," she greeted him, trying not to notice how the long-sleeved T-shirt hugged his wide shoulders and flat stomach. "Looks like you've been busy."

"There's a possibility of snow flurries tonight. I needed to get things done."

"Well, we're here to help. Grady, this is Mac and Connor Burleson."

The men shook hands and then quickly started with their tasks. The brothers loaded the two old sofas onto the truck bed, and went back for some smaller pieces that Grady had told her to take. In about thirty minutes the job was finished. Mac and Connor tied the furniture down, and then they were on their way back to town.

Back in the cabin, Gina began rearranging the furniture that was left behind. She placed the sofa toward the fireplace and tucked a large quilt over the back, then put a braided rug in front of it to cover the rough wooden floor. Since there was room now, she pulled the kitchen table away from the wall and placed a checkered tablecloth she found in the cupboard over the scarred surface.

She stood back and examined her work. "Not bad."

"It looks a helluva lot better than it did."

She turned to see Grady. "Sorry, I hope you don't mind that I moved some things around."

He shook his head. "No. You made it look so much

better and I can get around the room now. More importantly, my grandfather will be able to."

She thought it looked cozy. "Well, I should probably get back."

Grady looked at her. "If you have a few minutes, I've got something to show you."

Gina was surprised and intrigued. "Sure." She followed him out the door to the side of the cabin. That was where she saw a high fence and the small building.

"You built a kennel."

"It's temporary."

She saw Scout. He barked and came to the fence to greet her. Soon another shepherd came into view. A lighter color, more golden. "That's Beau." Then two others appeared. "And that's Rowdy and Bandit."

"Oh, Grady. They're beautiful. Can I pet them?"

"I want to work with those two awhile first." He gave a hand signal and the dogs sat, and he managed to retrieve the smaller shepherd named Bandit. Once outside, the lovable animal was all over her. "Well, aren't you a lover."

"Hey, stay back," Grady ordered. It worked, but the little guy began to whine when she moved away.

"I thought you were only getting two dogs."

"When I picked these two up at the Durango airport, my partner, Josh, told me about Bandit. He didn't complete the program, but I didn't want him to go into a shelter." Grady turned that dark gaze on her. "If you're serious about getting a dog for Zack, this guy would be a good one for him."

Gina looked back at the dog. He had the gold and black markings of a shepherd, with two circles around his eyes. "Is he safe for kids?"

"These dogs are socialized before they even start

with any other training. I'd never recommend him if he wasn't safe. Of course he needs a little discipline, but yes, he'd be a good companion dog for Zack. And a good watchdog for the house, too."

"Is Zack old enough to handle a big dog?"

"Owning any pet is work, Gina."

She was a little surprised when he said her name. He'd never been that personal before.

"If you have a yard, and can afford to feed him, Bandit will be a great dog for a child. But only if you feel you want a pet."

She refocused on the cute dog. "Okay. Okay, you sold me. What do I owe you for him?"

He shook his head. "Nothing, Josh and I are just glad that we could find him a home. I would like to hold on to Bandit for a few days, just to see what needs to be worked on. I'll bring him into town this weekend. Will you be home?"

"I work Saturday, so is Sunday okay?" At his nod, she went on to say, "Plan on staying for supper." She began to laugh like a silly girl. "Oh, Zack is going to be so excited, especially since you've picked him out. He hasn't stopped talking about Scout and you." She added silently that she'd done her fair share of thinking about this man, too.

Sunday afternoon Grady drove his truck off Main Street onto Cherry Street, a tree-lined street with well-kept family homes. The Williamses' house was a green clapboard bungalow with a large front yard and spring flowers that edged a big porch.

He pulled up to the curb and parked his truck and glanced around. This reminded him of another lifetime. He'd once had a home that looked a lot like this. It had taken them a while before he and Barbara had been able to get their first place, especially since the army had moved him around every few years.

Then he'd been stationed in Texas to stay for a two-year stint. But he hadn't stayed, he'd left to go back to fight a war. He closed his eyes, not wanting to remember the rest. Maybe because he wanted to forget the pain of a bad marriage, and the child he'd never know.

He leaned back against the headrest, recalling the whirlwind romance with the pretty blonde, Barbara Dixon. They'd met at a nightclub while he was on leave, he'd ended up going home with her, and had just stayed. They'd married within weeks, just days before he was deployed.

Nearly a year later he'd come home from overseas and found they were strangers. They were. In all fairness, he hadn't worked that hard at being as social as Barbara needed him to be. He'd tried over the next year to be as attentive as he could.

She struggled with him being gone so much, but he felt helpless to change it. Their marriage suffered for it. Then while deployed again in Afghanistan, Barbara shocked him with the news that he was going to be a father. Excited, he hoped to be home when his child arrived into the world. Then complications had set in and Barbara had gone into labor a month early. He'd got emergency leave, but by the time he arrived home, it was too late. He couldn't even share the loss with his wife. She wanted nothing to do with him. His son was gone. The marriage was over, maybe before it had even had a chance.

Grady shook away thoughts when he heard his name and looked to see Zack running toward the truck. Scout barked from the backseat, causing a chain reaction from Bandit.

"Okay, boys, I want you two on your best behavior." He climbed out of the truck. "Hey, Zack. How's it going?"

"Fine." He nodded toward the truck. "Who's with Scout?"

"What?" He turned and looked at the dogs. "Well, how did he get in my truck?" Grady opened the back door and signaled for Scout to come out. He was grateful that Bandit stayed, but obviously he wanted to get some attention, too.

"You call him out." Grady showed the boy a hand signal.

Zack motioned and Bandit jumped out of the truck. "I did it." He glanced over his shoulder. "Mom, did you see what I did?"

Gina walked up to them. "I saw. Boy, this sure is a pretty dog."

Grady could only stare at her. Gina Williams was the pretty one. She was dressed in jeans and a blue sweater, showing off her trim figure.

"What's his name?" Zack asked, drawing his attention back.

"This is Bandit."

"Wow! That's a cool name. Are you going to train him to rescue people, too?"

Grady shook his head. "No, I have Scout. And my two other dogs, Beau and Rowdy, are back at the cabin. This guy is pretty young and he needs a home."

"Really? Can anyone adopt him? I mean even a kid?"

Grady nodded again.

Zack looked at his mother. "Mom, can we adopt Bandit and have him live with us?"

She acted like she was thinking it over. "That depends. Are you sure this is the kind of dog you want?"

"Yes! He almost looks like Scout."

"A dog is a big responsibility."

Grady took over. "You'll need to feed him, Zack. Not just when you have time, but every morning and evening." He petted the shepherd. "He needs to be walked, and most importantly, clean up after him."

"Oh, I promise I will." He turned to his mother. "I really promise, Mom. Every day."

Something tightened in his chest. This boy had been through a lot in his short life. He had been braver than most adults. "Bandit will need his training reinforced."

Grady glanced at Gina. "He hasn't been worked with much. So he's not as good at taking orders as Scout."

The boy nodded. "I'll work with him, I promise."

Grady nodded. "Then I guess he's yours."

The boy threw his small arms around Grady. "Thank you, Grady. I promise I'll love him and take care of him."

"I know you will, son," he said, feeling a funny tightening in his chest.

Then Zack moved away and went to his mother and hugged her. "Oh, thank you, Mom."

Grady moved away from the touching scene and went to the truck bed and picked up a large bag of food and a dog bed.

There was the sound of a horn and he looked up to see an SUV pull up behind his truck. Gina's sister, Lori, got out, along with a man he recognized as Jace Yeager. A young girl climbed out of the backseat and went straight to Zack and Bandit.

So this was going to be a family dinner. Great.

The sisters hugged and Lori turned toward him. "It's good to see you again, Mr. Fletcher."

"It's Grady, ma'am," he said and saw the resemblance between the sisters. The hair and eye color might have been different, but the shape of the face, and the flawless skin was shared between the two sisters.

"I'm Lori, remember? This is my husband, Jace." The two men shook hands. "And that's our daughter, Cassie." Lori glanced at her husband. "Brace yourself, she's gonna want a dog now."

"She's got a horse," Jace argued.

The attention turned back to Grady and Lori said, "I don't think I ever thanked you for finding Zack."

"No need. I've been thanked enough."

"Maybe so, but I have to say it again. Thank you, Grady Fletcher." She quickly changed the subject. "How is your grandfather doing?"

"He seems to be recovering nicely."

"Is he up for visitors?"

"Who wants to see him?"

"I wanted to stop by and speak with him about some land that there's a question about."

"If this has anything to do with Billy Hutchinson, I'm not sure I want you stirring up any trouble."

"No trouble, Grady. It's righting a wrong that my grandfather did years ago. Once I took over the bank, I discovered a title to a piece of land that I believe belongs to Joe Fletcher. Maybe when he's feeling better I can correct this…mistake."

Gina stood back and watched the change in Grady's demeanor. How different he'd been with just Zack and her. Now that the group was bigger, he seemed tense. He wasn't comfortable around people.

Grady didn't have time to reflect on Lori Hutchinson

Yeager's confession as they herded both kids and dogs to the backyard. Grady followed Gina to put away the bag of dog food in the cupboard on the utility porch. The oversize dog bed was placed next to the clothes dryer.

"I doubt Bandit will be sleeping in here," she said. "I know Zack wants him to be in his bedroom."

Grady nodded. "This dog has been kenneled at night, but I'm sure there won't be a problem with Bandit sleeping in Zack's room. Just not in the bed."

"Okay, but you have to tell Zack, along with any other rules about caring for the dog."

"I will." He looked into her green eyes and started to get distracted. "How's Zack doing?"

"Better each day, but he still isn't sleeping in his own room. Jace is going to replace the windows and put in higher ones so Zack will feel safe again. Right now he's sleeping in another room that I've been using as my office." He saw her watery eyes. "And we have an appointment tomorrow to go and talk to a therapist about what happened."

Grady tensed. He'd love to get his hands on Lowell again. *Who does that to a child?* "He's gone through a lot. It'll take time."

He couldn't help but think about what Gina had gone through, too. The years of abuse from a man who claimed he loved her. "What about you? How are you handling this?"

She looked surprised at the question. "I'm okay, as long as Zack recovers from this."

The sounds of giggles coming from the backyard got Gina's attention. She smiled and his heart skipped a beat. "I guess having a dog is a start. Thank you."

"Not a problem," he told her, wondering why her praise meant so much to him.

"Come on, Grady, let's join the fun."

She started out the door, but he hesitated. It had been a long time since he'd done any family things. He'd never been very good at it. The army had been his family. And now he didn't even have that. He wasn't sure what he had.

An hour later Gina, Grady, Jace and Lori were sitting on the patio finishing their hamburgers while the kids played with the dogs.

Gina loved that her family was all together, at her house. She'd never expected to have someone like Grady Fletcher sit beside her, but he seemed on edge all during the meal. Finally he'd gotten up and taken Zack out to teach him how to work the dogs.

She glanced at her son, running around the yard with his dog. Zack was so happy.

Grady had given them some tricks to work on and that was all it took. The kids started burying things, and soon the dogs were retrieving toys and returning them. Bandit got distracted pretty easily, but some training would help that.

Gina's attention went to the ex-soldier standing alone. Did he have a problem being around a lot of people? She'd noticed how his demeanor had changed when her sister and her family had arrived.

Lori turned to her husband. "Mark my words, Cassie will ask for a puppy before we get back home."

"If you really want one, I bet Grady can find you one."

Jace groaned. "Don't give your niece any ideas." He hugged his wife. "We're hoping a new baby will distract her from wanting any more pets."

They all three laughed as the back gate opened and

Gina saw Claire and Tim Keenan walk in. Gina rushed over to greet them both with a hug.

"I hope we're not intruding," Claire said, holding out a covered dish.

Gina hugged the two. "Claire and Tim, of course you're not, you're always welcome. Please, join us."

"Oh, no, we just wanted to drop off this pie and tell you how happy we are that both you and Zack are back safe."

"I insist you stay. We're about to have some coffee and now some pie."

"I can go for that," Tim volunteered as they walked toward the others on the patio.

Gina introduced Grady, letting him know they owned the Keenan Inn, a historical bed-and-breakfast in town.

"Sheriff Larkin is married to their daughter, Paige, who is an attorney. Their oldest daughter, Morgan, is the mayor. Their youngest daughter, Leah, is a photo journalist. They all came back to Destiny to raise their families."

After they shook hands, Tim said, "Sounds like a Chamber of Commerce ad." The older man smiled. "I remember you, but it's been a while. You were just a kid. Old Fletch used to come into town and bring you along."

Gina watched as Grady nodded. "That wasn't very often," he admitted. "He didn't like people much."

So that was where he got it from. Was Grady a loner like his grandfather, or was it the scar?

Tim Keenan laughed. "No, he didn't. Most of the old miners kept to themselves. I think they were afraid someone would jump their claims if they left them for long."

Grady gave a rare smile. "Yeah, I used to hear a lot

of those stories. I feel bad I wasn't around to help him more."

Claire added, "Rest assured, the Shady Haven Nursing Home is a wonderful facility. I volunteer there, so I see how happy their patients are." She smiled. "I hope you don't mind, but I stop in to see your grandfather from time to time."

"I appreciate it." Grady was ashamed that his own personal problems had interfered with spending more time with his grandfather. "I didn't get to see much of him the past few years."

Claire smiled. "Fletch understood, and let us know on more than one occasion that you were defending our freedom," she told him. "And we, too, thank you for your service."

He nodded. "I'm retired now."

Tim stepped in. "I hear you're already starting a new career, training dogs for search and rescue." He looked out toward the shepherds. "Are those two of them?"

"Just the one," Grady said as he pointed to the bigger dog. "That's Scout."

"He found Zack," Gina added. "The other younger one is Bandit, he's Zack's new dog."

Claire looked from Gina toward Grady. "That's really nice of you to get the boy such a special dog. Are you planning to move here permanently?"

"No. I'm going back to Texas once Fletch is settled and on his feet again."

"Oh, do you have family there?"

Grady knew where this was going. Mrs. Keenan was already putting Gina and him together as a couple. "No, it's just me." He glanced around. He needed to leave, and soon.

Suddenly as if Gina saw his distress, she interrupted.

"Oh, we need some plates for our dessert," she said, then rushed into the house.

Grady knew that he couldn't get away as easily. What was he thinking, getting involved with them? He wanted to come here and sit on the mountain while his grandfather recuperated. Why couldn't he be left alone?

Over the past several nights his solitude had been invaded by a lost boy and a beautiful single mother. None of which he needed at this point in his life. Probably never. Gina Williams had her own issues. So did he. She needed a patient guy who wanted a family. Grady didn't do family. He'd tried and failed, never again. He'd stick with animals.

"They're beautiful dogs." Tim Keenan came up to him. "Were they overseas, too?"

"Scout was. He's completed his service so I was able to adopt him. Bandit didn't make the program, but he's still an excellent dog."

"Even better that Zack gets to have one, too." Tim shook his head. "That boy has been through hell, and he was just starting to open up when this all happened. I think Bandit will be a great therapy dog for him."

"I'm glad I could help. I need to get back before dark." He stood and whistled for Scout. The dog stopped then ran toward him and sat. Grady said goodbye to everyone as he started to leave.

"Don't be a stranger in town," Tim said as he walked with him to the gate. "Get to know people here in Destiny. You'll find we're pretty easy to get along with."

Grady just wasn't sure he wanted to form any attachments. He'd be leaving soon. Definitely the best idea before he got distracted by one pretty brunette.

CHAPTER SIX

THREE days later Gina stood at the front window of her shop on First Street. The Second Best Thrift Shop had an ideal location right off the town square.

She could see the large fountain and park, along with several other storefront shops. Destiny Community Bank was across the street, next door was Paige Keenan Larkin's law office and the Rocky Mountain Bridal Shop. The sheriff's office was on the next block along with the U.S. post office.

Gina had been lucky to get a space in a prime location. The front of the shop was her thrift store. The showroom was still a little sparse, but once she cleaned up the pieces she'd gotten from Grady Fletcher, it should add a lot to the window display.

Her thoughts turned to the man who had upset her tranquillity. She still didn't know much about the ex-army master sergeant who lived on the mountain. Only that he'd seen war, and had to have suffered greatly with his obvious burns. She'd seen the pain in his eyes. Yet, from the way he stood back from people, she somehow doubted it was all physical.

Still he hadn't hesitated to help find Zack. That alone made Grady Fletcher pretty special. The part that bothered her was that she found she was drawn to him.

She'd spent just over twenty-four hours with the man, and oddly, she felt safe around him. Given her past record with men, she hadn't found it easy to trust. And she might never find it easy.

She couldn't help but recall the width of Grady's shoulders and chest. Her breath caught in her throat as she remembered his gentle touch, with her, Zack and his dogs.

She shook away the direction of her thoughts. She was in no way ready to think about a man in her life. Besides, Grady Fletcher would be leaving for Texas soon. That right there should make her keep her distance. Not that he would ever want her, not with all her baggage. Not with her fears of intimacy. She could never measure up to what Eric wanted in a wife or a lover. He'd let her know time and again that she couldn't please him.

She shook away the memories. No, she didn't need a man. She was happy with her life as it was. She was independent and had her family.

Most importantly, Zack. This was his first day back to school since the ordeal. Even though she'd talked with her son about the situation, she knew it would be a long time before he got over the events of those harrowing twenty-four hours. Their new dog helped a lot.

She smiled, thinking about Bandit. He'd been the best medicine ever. Boy and dog had been inseparable the past two days. So there had been sad faces this morning when she'd taken Zack to school. Maybe she should go home at lunch to check on Bandit, just to make sure he was okay.

Gina checked her watch. Right, she needed to get to work herself, so she walked toward the back of her store. In the work area she saw the two sofas from Grady's cabin. Marie, her young helper, was already removing the dirty, worn fabric.

"How bad is it, Marie?" she asked the young mother of a twelve-month-old little girl, Sophie.

The tall, willowy blonde was about Gina's age. She had an easy smile and a real talent with a sewing machine.

"Not bad. The frame is solid and with new padding and fabric it will look great."

"That's what I was thinking when I saw it." Gina grinned. "And it was free." She eyed the other sofa. "How about you reupholster this one, and I'll do the camelback sofa? Since I can't pay you what you're really worth, how about you take sixty percent of the sale?"

"Oh, Gina, you don't have to do that."

"Yes, I do. I'm barely paying you now. And don't tell me you can't use the money."

Marie's husband was finishing college and could only work part time. "But how many bosses let an employee bring her kid to work?"

Not many that Gina knew of, remembering when she herself had tried to find work with Zack in tow. "Hey, a business should supply a daycare, even if it is a small storage area in the back of the store."

"It's perfect. And thank you for that."

"Let's just get these sofas finished so we can sell 'em."

Marie looked toward the wide doorway that led out to the alley. "I think we have a visitor."

Gina turned around. She couldn't be more surprised to find Grady Fletcher. He looked big and intimidating. Did he do that on purpose?

She put on a smile and went to him. "Grady. It's nice to see you again."

He gave her a nod and stepped through the doorway as if he wouldn't be welcome. "Didn't mean to disturb you, but I thought I'd come around back to drop off some things I found in the shed."

"Oh, really?" Gina glanced over her shoulder. "Marie this is Grady Fletcher. Grady, Marie, my jack-of-all-trades."

"Nice to meet you, Grady."

Grady tipped his cowboy hat. "Ma'am."

He turned his attention back to Gina, causing her to feel nervous. "As you can see, we've started tearing apart the sofas you gave me."

He walked over. His gaze searched the furniture. She wondered if that was how he looked when he inspected the troops.

"Looks like a lot of work."

"It'll be worth it once they're finished. Right, Marie?"

"Right," the pretty blonde agreed. Gina planned to put them in the front display window. She put on a big smile. "Of course, they won't be there long, once we work our magic."

"Well, good luck with that."

Gina pulled his attention back. "You said you have some more furniture?"

Grady nodded, wondering what he was doing here. One look at Gina Williams, and already he was distracted. She looked fresh, young and so pretty. Dressed in those nice-fitting jeans and a denim blouse, she could pass for a teenager. Too young for him. And it seemed every time he got near her, he couldn't seem to act normal.

"I was clearing out the shed when I found some

things." He pointed over his shoulder. "They're in the truck."

She smiled and his heart began to pound hard. "May I see them?"

"Sure."

They walked out to his truck. Scout spotted her and barked in greeting from the backseat.

"Well, hello, fella." When the dog stuck his head out the open window, she went to him and began to pet him. "Oh, I know a little boy who misses you," she told the animal.

"How is Zack doing?"

She turned to him. "Good. He went back to school today, but as a mother, I worry. What if the kids start saying things? Teasing him?"

Grady leaned against the truck door, then realized he was close enough to inhale her soft scent. "I would think the kids would be more interested in Zack spending the night in a silver mine, more than his dad kidnapping him."

She looked up with those moss-green eyes. "Thank you for that, but I can't help but be overprotective."

"You have good reason to be. But now, you know you and your son are safe from your ex."

She sighed. "You can't imagine how good that feels. We can finally concentrate on making a life for ourselves."

He wondered if that included finding someone to share that life. It wouldn't take long for the men in this town to come sniffing around.

She smiled. "Like you are," she added.

He nodded, but he wasn't sure what his permanent plans were. "Thanks to my grandfather I have a place to live for now. On the downside, Old Fletch is a packrat—my immediate future is filled with a lot of work clearing out the place."

"Your grandfather is a man after my own heart." She rubbed her hands together excitedly. "So what did you bring me?"

He couldn't help but smile. "I don't know if this stuff is even worth bringing in." He walked to the truck bed and unfastened the tarp and pulled it back, then let down the gate.

"Oh, my," she said, and began to climb up on the bumper. Grady reached out, gripped her waist and boosted her up into the truck.

Gina froze momentarily, but then realized this was Grady touching her. She trusted him—as much as she would ever trust a man—not to hurt her. What truly scared her were the feelings that he did stir in her.

She quickly concentrated on the treasures he'd brought her. Another rocking chair, a cedar trunk, a Tiffany lamp. But it was a small pedestal table that got her attention. She pulled back the tarp further and was rewarded with a leather top in nearly perfect condition.

"Where did you find all this?"

"Buried in the shed out back." He climbed up and stood next to her. "Why?"

Gina examined it more closely, pulling out the single drawer to see the name stamped inside. "It a Mersman pedestal table with a leather top." She ran her fingers over the camel-colored softness. "How is it in such perfect condition?"

"Like I said, it was protected by a tarp and buried under a lot of stuff. I think it belonged to my grandmother. Maybe after she died, Fletch just put her things away."

She gave him a questioning look. "Are you sure your grandfather is okay about selling these things?"

"I saw him yesterday. He agreed that the cabin needs to be cleared out. He gave me first pick on these things. Except his bed. He wants me to keep my hands off that bed."

She smiled. "Your grandfather seems to be quite a character."

"Joe Fletcher was a miner, which wasn't an easy life. He once lived in Destiny, but after my grandmother passed away, he moved up to the cabin to work his claim. My father didn't like the life there so he didn't hang around after he turned eighteen. He didn't come back here much, either." Only to drop his kid off so he didn't have to deal with him, he added silently.

Gina studied him. "But you like it here."

"Old Fletch wasn't so bad." Their gazes locked, and he found himself saying more than he'd planned. "I was sent to spend my summers here after my parents divorced."

"It's nice you had him, but it must have been hard…" Her face brightened, and he could hardly draw a breath. "I bet those times were fun."

Yeah, he loved the old guy. "No one taught me more." He glanced around at the mountain range. "I hiked this area a lot of summers."

"Must be some nice memories," she said and sighed. "I want that for Zack. I want him to be able to erase all the bad that has happened to him."

Grady studied her pretty face. He found the need to reach out and touch her, but he fought the attraction. Making any kind of connection was a bad idea. "You have a good start here."

"I hope so," she said. "And I bet Fletch is happy that you're back here."

Honestly, he'd always felt a connection to this place. "Since the army sent me packing, I need to make a living. So it's back to Texas and my business."

She nodded. "But you have family here. I learned it's not the structure that makes it a home, it's the people. My son and my sister are my family, and we added Jace and Cassie. I'm lucky to have all of them."

This discussion was getting far too involved. "Yes, you are. Look, I need to get going. Scout has been in the truck a long time."

"Oh, of course. Just tell me what you want me to do about the table. Do you want to sell it on consignment? I'm not sure I can afford to buy it outright."

He moved the table to the end of the truck bed, then jumped down. He needed to put some distance between them. "Whatever you decide. I just need to clear out things to make room for when Fletch comes home."

Gina nodded. "How about I clean it up for you?" she suggested. "You might want to keep it. After all, it belonged to your grandmother."

"Whatever. You can go ahead and sell the trunk and rocker."

They moved the items out of the truck bed, then he helped her down. He didn't want to make a big deal about touching her, but when he put his hands on her tiny waist, his reaction became one. As hard as he tried, they ended up too close. Then their eyes met and he saw she was just as affected as he was. Great.

He placed her on the ground and she stumbled. He reached out and pulled her to him before she fell. Her softness pressed against his body was torture, the best kind.

"Ah, sorry." She regained her balance and moved back. Way back. "If you help me get these things inside, then you can be on your way."

He didn't say a word, realizing it had been a bad idea to come here in the first place. He needed to stay away from Gina Williams.

As he lifted the table off the truck, Marie came out. She called to Gina, "The school called."

"Oh, no. Did something happen with Zack?"

The blonde smiled. "No, but it seems he has a visitor. His name is Bandit."

Ten minutes later Gina and Grady with Scout on a leash headed to the school office. He'd brought the dog along in case they needed some extra support to corral Bandit.

A middle-aged principal came outside to greet her. "Hello, Ms. Williams."

"Hello, Mr. Markham. This is Grady Fletcher.

"Mr. Fletcher." The principal nodded, then turned back to Gina. "It seems your son's dog came to school."

"I'm so sorry, Mr. Markham. The last I checked Bandit was in the backyard." She looked at Grady. "How could he find his way to the school?"

Grady answered, "Either he followed the scent, or the sound of the kids' voices. He has more potential than I thought."

Gina didn't care how the dog got there. Just that she had a problem if he kept getting out of the yard.

"Well according to Zack," Markham began, "Bandit is a very smart dog. Outside of a German shepherd named Scout, Bandit is the smartest dog in the whole world. And he was in the army."

"Meet Scout," Grady said and Gina noticed a hint of

a smile. "I'm the one who gave Bandit to Zack. Where is the dog now?"

"Zack is with him on the playground."

Together they all walked back to the area behind the building. "Mr. Fletcher," the principal began, "Zack has told me a lot about your dogs, Beau, Rowdy and Scout. He said you're training them to be search-and-rescue dogs."

"I've only been working with Scout so far." He glanced down at his obedient shepherd. "He's coming along. Bandit hasn't had as much training. But I'm thinking he should get a gold star for finding little boys now."

"We all hear that Scout found Zack when he was lost," the man said.

Grady nodded. "He played a big part in it."

The principal caught Gina's attention. "I know you and your son have been through a rough time this past week."

Gina hated that everyone knew what had happened. She'd hoped that she could leave her past behind in Colorado Springs. "Yes, we have. Thank you for understanding."

The man nodded. "I noticed how much Zack responded when his dog showed up today. Even though I can't have Bandit at school every day, maybe a little show-and-tell with the two dogs wouldn't hurt."

Grady hesitated, then said, "After today, I'm not sure Bandit is ready for prime time."

"Maybe in a few weeks then?"

"We'll see."

They reached the playground and found the boy and the dog along with Claire Keenan, an aid from the class.

Zack spotted her. "Mom!" he cried and came running to her. "Mom, look, Bandit found my school. He followed my scent. He came to my classroom door. He really did."

"I heard," she said, wondering how to fix this problem. She looked at Mrs. Keenan. "Claire, thank you so much for staying with them."

"Oh, I was happy to do it." She looked at Grady. "Hi, Grady. It's nice to see you again."

"Hello, ma'am."

The older woman smiled. "I just love how respectful these soldiers are. But you can just call me Claire."

He nodded then snapped a leash on Bandit. "Thanks, Claire."

Mrs. Keenan was starting to leave, then stopped. "We're having a little get-together Sunday afternoon at the inn, just family and friends. We would love it if you all would join us."

"Thank you, Claire," Gina said. "That would be nice."

The older woman looked at Grady. "You could bring Scout, and Zack can bring Bandit. There's a wooded area behind the inn—maybe you can work the dogs. The kids would love it."

Grady was barely able to keep from squirming. Great, the good citizens of Destiny were trying to bring him into the fold. "Thank you for the invitation."

"Any time. We want you to feel a part of this community."

That was the problem. He wasn't sure if he wanted to be part of anything. "I'll try and make it."

"It's an open invitation, Grady." Claire walked back into the classroom, with a promise from Gina that she'd bring Zack.

Zack's smile faded as he looked up at Grady. "Is Bandit in trouble?"

"He's your dog, son. But I suggest he has some reinforcing discipline. It sounds harsh but you don't want Bandit to get hit by a car—which he might do if he's forever wandering about the town. So it looks like you'll need to work with him. Teach him his boundaries."

Gina watched as her son leaned against the dog in question. The two were already so close.

"Will you help me, Grady?" Zack asked. "I want Bandit to be as smart as Scout."

Grady went down to Zack's level. "Then he needs *you* to teach him. You need to show him who is the leader of the pack."

"I don't know what that means."

"It means you're the boss."

Gina watched the exchange between the two. Her son was hanging on to every word Grady said. Even with Lori's husband, Jace, it had taken Zack a long time to warm up to him. Not true with this man. She wasn't sure if that was a good thing.

"Hey, Mom, I'm the boss of Bandit."

"Well, right now, I'm the boss. And you need to go back to class. So say goodbye to Bandit."

Her son hugged the dog, then stopped in front of Grady. "Will you come to my house and teach me how to be the boss?"

Gina held her breath. She didn't want to step into this, even though she knew that Grady had done so much for them. More than she could ever repay.

"How about I make sure the backyard is secured?" he told the boy. "I'll give you some exercises to help show Bandit his boundaries. But you have to do the work."

That seemed to make her son happy. "Okay."

Gina saw the change in Grady from earlier when he'd opened up to her. Were they becoming too much of a burden? Of course they were. Grady was a single man who didn't need a kid hanging on him. She kissed her son goodbye and watched him head off to class.

The ride back to her house with Grady was a silent one. When she climbed out of the truck with Bandit in tow, she expected Grady to drive off. Instead he followed them to the backyard. He searched the area until he found the hole under the fence where the dog had escaped.

"Do you have any extra wood?"

"There's some in the garage."

When he started to walk off, she tied Bandit to the post and went after Grady. "You don't have to fix it. I can do it."

"Not a problem."

She unlocked the door to the structure, turned on the light and led him to the neatly stacked boards that Jace had left after doing some house repairs.

"This is only a temporary fix," he told her.

"Then let me help," she insisted.

"There's no need." He started past her, but she refused to be ignored as she followed him.

"There's every need. I'm not helpless," she argued, then suddenly ran into the back of the man's hard body.

With a gasp, she backed away.

The wood hit the ground as Grady cursed and turned around.

His gaze met hers. "You okay?"

She nodded. "I'm sorry, I didn't know you were going to stop."

He just stood there staring at her, those dark eyes piercing.

"I don't know why, but I've made you angry."

He glanced away, then back at her. "I'm not angry at you, Gina. I'm angry with myself."

"Why?"

He took a step closer to her. "Because I can't stop thinking about doing this." He leaned down and his mouth closed over hers.

CHAPTER SEVEN

GINA jumped back quickly. "Why'd you do that?" She fought to keep her composure.

Grady shrugged. "Hell if I know."

"Well, next time try to control yourself."

"I'll be sure I do that." He turned, grabbed the long piece of wood and stalked out of the garage.

Gina sagged against the workbench and tried to slow her breathing. She ran her tongue over her lips. Oh, God. She could still taste him. Stop. It was only a kiss.

No. She wasn't going to get involved with a man. Not again. Never again. She already had the life she wanted for her and Zack. She didn't need a man in it. Besides, who would want to deal with all her hang-ups? She was so afraid of being touched, she'd never have a normal relationship.

She thought back to her old life. Eric had never treated her like anything but an object. She'd met him as a teenager when she had been so eager for attention. At that time, she'd been willing to do anything to have someone love her. Problem was, she'd confused sex with love, and had let Eric talk her into whatever he wanted. He never cared about her, only the power he had over her. And then the control had begun.

Too late, she'd realized she'd never had a voice about

anything. At nearly nineteen, she'd become a bride and a mother. She knew nothing. When Eric had started pushing her around she was too ashamed to tell anyone. It had been Lori who had rescued her and Zack.

Even after counseling, she still had trouble with self-esteem, especially when it came to men. Could she handle a man's touch? She wondered if she'd ever be able to enjoy the physical part of a relationship. Could she hold the interest of a man like Grady Fletcher? As good looking as the man was, he had to be used to women's attention, experienced women. She was far from knowing how to please a man...how to keep a man.

Gina walked to the garage doorway and looked out. She saw Grady as he knelt down at the base of the fence and went to work at boarding up Bandit's escape route. Big and muscular, she had no doubt Grady was a take-charge guy. Yet, he'd never made her feel any fear. She touched her lips with her fingertips. The yearning was still there, making her want something she couldn't have. A normal relationship with a man.

Thirty minutes later Grady drove his truck along the dirt road to the cabin, still cursing his bad judgment. Damn! Why couldn't he just keep his hands off Gina? He didn't need this complication. He'd come back here to take some time to heal and rebuild his life. He didn't need Gina Williams distracting him, making him want things again. Especially not a woman with a child reminding him of everything he'd lost.

Grady parked the truck in front of the cabin and climbed out. He got Scout from the backseat and walked up to the porch. After unlocking the door, he went inside and glanced around at Gina's handiwork.

A woman's touch. Something he'd taken for granted

during his marriage. Even though he and Barbara had been together only four years, he'd got used to coming home to all the comforts. Even with the short time they'd had together as a couple, he'd missed the things that only a woman could give.

In the end, he hadn't been there enough. Okay, so she had signed on as a career army wife, but two tours of duty overseas during a marriage had taken a toll.

Although he'd warned her, Barbara still hadn't deserved the heartache. He'd given it a hundred percent when he was stateside, but that hadn't been enough to make it work. He'd learned too late—he was never the marrying kind. He should have saved them both the heartache.

He walked into the cabin's one bedroom and went to the scarred dresser, then opened the top drawer and took out a small box. The only thing he'd taken from his home after the divorce. He felt his heart begin to pound and his hands shook as he raised the lid on the treasure box he'd had since he'd been a kid. But it was what was inside that tore him apart. He looked down at the grainy photo. The only picture he had of his son.

A sonogram.

Grady sank onto the bed as he studied the image of a child that had never been born.

He took a shaky breath, wondering if this sad helpless feeling would ever leave him. The feeling that told him he'd served his country proudly, but couldn't get home to help his family. Of course, if he'd known that Barbara had been pregnant before volunteering, he might have thought twice about going back overseas. He remembered the weekly phone calls he'd made home and hearing about the pregnancy, then later when the commanding officer had given him the news that his wife was in the hospital. He'd managed to get on the first plane home. But it was too late. Worse, Barb blamed him for everything, but not nearly as much as he blamed himself.

He quickly shook away the memory.

His thoughts turned to Gina. No! He wasn't getting involved with her. She needed a man who would be there for her. A normal man without battle scars, who was able to give her what she needed. Treat her how she needed to be treated, special. Give her a home and a life of happiness.

Hell, he wasn't sure what his future would be. He had a grandfather who needed to be cared for. A cabin in the mountains that didn't even have a flushing toilet. He'd had no business kissing her. He needed to stay away from both mother and child.

Scout barked then raced out of the bedroom. Then Grady heard, "Hello, is anyone here?"

"Who the hell?" Grady quickly put the box back into the drawer and hurried through the cabin to find the intruder leaning down and petting the shepherd in the open doorway.

"Hey, Sarge, you shouldn't leave your door open," the man said.

Grady recognized the army corporal right away. Twenty-seven-year-old Josh Regan had served in his unit overseas. They'd both survived the explosion that day that had taken out two of their squad members. They'd spent time in the hospital where they'd been treated for wounds and burns. That was where they'd come up with the idea of training dogs.

"Hey, partner. What are you doing here?"

"Well, I figured I'd stop by and see how you're getting along with the dogs."

Grady couldn't help but smile. "Not too bad. I thought you were headed home to Georgia for a visit with your family and your girl."

The tall, lanky Southern boy straightened. "I've been home and discovered there isn't a girl waiting any longer." He sighed. "So after chowin' down enough of my mother's cooking, I thought I'd stop by here to see you and the dogs and firm up our plans before I headed back to Texas." Regan looked around. "So this is the place you talked about... Nice digs."

"Livable. The view is the best." He studied the kid. "I told you the last time we talked, Josh, I can't leave yet." They'd planned the partnership, but then that had been delayed when his grandfather had ended up in the hospital. "I'm not sure when I'll get back to Texas."

"I know that. I just thought I'd take a detour before heading back to Lackland. Maybe I can hang around for a few days and we can work with the dogs."

The idea was a good one. He could get some work done on the cabin and not neglect the dogs. "I should have thought about that. We could work here for now. The cabin is short on guest quarters, but you're welcome to bunk on the sofa."

Regan seemed to relax. "You sure?"

"Wouldn't offer if I wasn't. Besides, I could use a hand with the training here, and you're the expert handler."

A big boyish grin appeared. "I've got a sleeping bag in my truck. Then I'll go visit with Beau and Rowdy."

Josh followed Grady out to the porch. He pointed over his shoulder. "I have built some makeshift kennels for now, but we might need something sturdier if we're going to work on training."

The corporal stopped and looked around at the view. "I could get used to this great view."

It was a great view, but their training facility was in Texas. "Yeah, but it's still my grandfather's cabin and he's dead set on returning here once the doctor releases him."

Josh let out a long breath. "Too bad. I could get used to the cooler weather."

Grady couldn't help but smile, too. It was good to see a familiar face. Someone who had been through the same things and understood. "Well, you're not going to get the chance to sit around and enjoy it. We'll be working."

"That's why I'm here. To help out."

And Grady was glad. They could get some things done, and it would keep him from thinking about a pretty brunette who was too young and fragile for him. He glanced at his partner and realized Josh was better suited for Gina. Yet, he didn't want the man anywhere near her.

"Don't think I don't know what you're up to."

The next morning, Grady sat across from his grandfather at Shady Haven. "Okay, what am I up to?"

The older man glared. "You're cleaning up the cabin, then you're going to clear out as soon as I get out of this place."

Grady sighed. "You always knew I was headed back to Texas, but I'm not going to leave you until you can make it on your own. You still need rehab on your hip. That means you can't return to the cabin, especially with so much stuff crammed into the place."

"I did just fine before," Joe said, his dark eyes narrowed as he raised his large, veined hand. "I know where everything is."

"So you want me to put everything back? That might be hard to do since Gina Williams carted most of it off."

The old man frowned. "Who is Gina?"

"She runs the thrift store in town."

"You kept my bed, didn't you?"

"Didn't touch your bed. But Gina wants to know about some of Grandma's things."

Joe eyed him closely. "Seems you're spending a lot of time with this woman. Are you sweet on her?"

Grady wasn't sure how to handle this one. "No, I'm not. I don't have the time for a woman. Besides, you know I don't do so well in relationships."

"You would if you picked the right one." There was a hint of a smile. "Bring this Gina by here. And I'll tell you if she's good enough for you."

"Look, Fletch, don't you think I'm too old to have your approval on who I see."

"Ha, ha. So you are seeing her," he said, then he sobered. "Don't be too stubborn to see what's right in front of you, boy. Take it from one who knows. Time slips by fast. So make an old man happy, and bring your young lady by."

Grady knew it would be foolish if he did bring Gina here. "I'll see what I can do."

Sunday afternoon, the Keenan Inn was the place to be, especially if you liked to be around family, friends and good food.

Gina got out of the car followed by Zack just as another vehicle pulled up behind her. She immediately recognized Grady and it sent her heart racing. She'd known he was going to be here, but she still wasn't ready to see him again.

"They're here, Mom. Grady and Scout are here."

Before she could stop him, her eager son grabbed Bandit's leash and raced off toward the truck as Grady climbed out. It had been a few days since the incident in the garage, and their kiss. The feel of his firm mouth against hers, his scent stirring her emotions. It was still fresh in her mind.

The man was hard to forget. His mere size and presence demanded her attention. Yet, she'd never been frightened by him, even by those dark, piercing eyes. He looked good. She knew he was self-conscious about the scar along his neck, but she didn't even notice it anymore.

She inhaled a calming breath and walked over to him. His gaze caught hers and held, refusing to let her look away. Then finally he spoke. "Hello, Gina."

"Hi, Grady," she managed to say.

Zack caught her attention. "Mom, can I go hide some stuff so Scout and Bandit can find it?"

"In a minute," she said, noticing another man getting out of the passenger side of the truck. He was younger with dark hair that had the familiar military cut.

"Gina," Grady began, "this is Josh Regan. We served together. He's also my partner in training the dogs. He's staying with me for a while."

The younger man said, "Hello, ma'am."

"It's nice to meet you, Josh. Please call me Gina. This is my son, Zack, and Bandit."

Josh smiled. "It's good to meet you both."

"Are you in the army, too?" Zack asked.

"I was. I served under Sgt. Fletcher. I was a dog handler."

"Wow! Cool."

Grady stood back and watched how Regan's attention remained on Gina. Okay, she was pretty enough to be stared at, but not as if she was his next meal.

"Hey, Josh." Grady handed him the dog leash. "Would you mind taking Scout out back and getting the kids organized on the exercise? I'll be there in a few."

"Sure." The younger guy didn't question the order and walked off with Zack and the dogs. Grady turned back to Gina. Oh, Lord, she looked good. "How have you been?"

"I'm fine."

He watched her, seeing her cheeks redden. Was she thinking about the kiss? He quickly asked, "I meant, how have you and Zack been?"

"He's back in his own bedroom."

"That's good." Enough small talk, he needed to clear the air. "Gina, about the other day... I was out of line. I promise it won't happen again."

"Let's just say we were both caught up in the situation..." She glanced away. "I just didn't want you to get any ideas. It's not that you're not attractive. I mean, any woman would want your attention." She shook her head. "It's just I'm not ready, nor do I want to get involved with anyone."

Grady heard her words of refusal, but that didn't change the fact that he was still drawn to her. "I can understand you feeling that way, but never is a long time. You're too young, Gina. There's a guy out there for you. Not all are jerks like your ex." He turned and headed toward the backyard of the inn.

Gina released a breath. The last thing she needed was Sgt. Fletcher telling her to date. She liked her life just fine as it was. She walked up the steps at the inn. She had her son and business to concentrate on. Grady had his own work, too. They should both be able to keep out of each other's way.

Resigned to keeping her distance from the man, Gina walked through the double doors with the glass oval panels, etched with the Keenan name. Inside, she stood in the entry with the antique desk used for registering guests at the historic bed-and-breakfast.

She glanced around at the high ceiling trimmed with crown moldings and wainscoting stained in a honey color. The walls were painted a light tan and the floors were covered in a burgundy carpet. The large polished oak staircase led to the second and third floors.

"Welcome."

Gina turned and found Tim Keenan. The handsome sixty-year-old offered her a ready smile that reached all the way to his clear blue eyes.

"Hi, Tim."

He walked up and hugged her. "Gina, so glad you could make it today. We don't see enough of you or your boy. Where is Zack?"

She stepped back. "He's headed out back with Grady and the dogs. I came in to see if I can help Claire."

"I think we have enough hands in that kitchen, but let's head back and ask them."

Tim and Gina walked through the dining room, which had several small tables for guests.

"How is Zack handling things these days?"

"Better," Gina told him. "He had a few sessions with a counselor." She smiled as they continued their journey through a butler's pantry. "I seem to be the one with the problem."

Gina was still a little overwhelmed by what had happened with the kidnapping and how close she'd come to losing her son. Yet Zack had seemed to fit right back into school and with the other kids. She was glad about that.

"I think as parents, Gina," Tim began, "we always worry about doing everything right for our kids. We can't. We just do our best and from what I see you are a great mom."

Gina felt the emotions building. "Not always. I made so many mistakes…with Eric. My son had to pay for that."

The big Irishman drew her into his arms again. "Oh, lass. You've got to forgive yourself and move on." In his tight embrace, she wondered if this was how girls felt having a father who cared about them. "You and Zack are safe here and Eric will never hurt either of you again."

"We're going to try." She pulled back, embarrassed by the tears in her eyes. "Sorry, I didn't mean to get so emotional on you."

He grinned. "Not at all. Now, our youngest, Leah, is the emotional one in the family. Always loved drama. Of course if you say anything, I'll deny it." He winked. "Come on, let's join the others."

They were greeted by the sound of voices first, then when the door opened, Gina saw several women working together in the huge kitchen, which was divided into two areas, a prep station for cooking and a dining area.

The Keenan daughters, Morgan, Paige and Leah, were helping their mother. There was a large picture window behind the table and she could see a group of kids running around the yard. The men were standing together talking as they watched the children.

Gina felt a different kind of emotion. Maybe a little

panic. She'd heard from Lori that Claire Keenan had played matchmaker more than once.

They were all paired off in couples. Except her and Grady. Of course Josh made it an odd number. Good.

"Grady should open a day care," Paige said as she nodded to the group of children. "Look how he's handling those kids. They aren't moving a muscle, just glued to his every word. Who knew all that military training would come in so handy?"

Morgan stepped in. "Maybe he can share some pointers on giving orders."

Gina turned her attention to Grady Fletcher. Okay so she was drawn to the man whether she liked it or not. Big and strong, he held your attention by his mere presence. The years of military training were engrained in the man. He demanded respect and he got it. From the kids and his dogs.

"Gina! You made it."

She turned to see Claire Keenan crossing the large kitchen to greet her. After a big hug, the older woman stepped back. "You look lovely."

Gina glanced down at her dark slacks and cream-colored sweater. "Thank you."

"Since I haven't seen Bandit at school again, I guess you fixed the escape route."

Gina nodded. "Grady repaired the fence. And he gave Zack some ideas on keeping the dog home."

Claire looked out at the yard. "That man seems to have a lot of talents. We just need to convince him to stay here." The older woman looked back at Gina. "We need another nice addition to our town, like you and Zack."

"Well, we sure love it here. And Second Best is doing great."

Claire smiled. "I hear you're doing some reupholstering."

Word spread fast in Destiny. "Grady was very generous and gave me a few items from his grandfather's cabin. I'm selling some other things for him, too."

"It's about time someone cleared out some of Joe's... treasures." Claire turned to the window. "I'm also glad that Fletch has his grandson around to help with his recovery." She nodded toward the window. "It also seems he's pretty good with the kids, too. That's something special in a man."

Gina had to agree. "Yes, he is." That was all she said as she walked outside. She leaned against the railing on the deck and watched as Grady talked with Zack. She saw the happiness and respect in her child's eyes. Except for Lori's new husband, Jace, her son had never had a man to look up to.

Then Eric had found them, tried to destroy their happiness. She'd worried that Zack would pull back again, but it looked like her boy had survived, and her ex-husband hadn't won.

Best of all, with numerous charges against him, kidnapping, attempted murder and resisting arrest, he would never be a threat again. Sheriff Larkin was going to make sure that he got everything he deserved. Maybe life was turning out to be something to look forward to.

Once again, her attention went to Grady. Darn if the man wasn't one big distraction. It was a good thing his visit was temporary. Now all she had to do was stay away from him until he left town. She could do that.

CHAPTER EIGHT

GRADY stood at the edge of the yard and watched as Josh took over exercising the dogs. The kids were so into it, and did exactly what they were told to do.

Scout didn't let them down after only one sniff of a small stuffed toy. Two of the older kids had been sent off to bury it, then using only their scent, Josh harnessed Scout and they went into the wooded area and soon returned with the correct items.

Morgan's husband, Justin Hilliard, came up to Grady. "I'm impressed," he told him.

Grady nodded. "Scout's been well trained."

"Does he work in snow?"

Grady continued to pet the shepherd. "Since we didn't arrive here until February, there's been limited opportunity to train, but we did a bit of tracking in the snow. I'm forever surprised how well these animals adapt to different climates."

Justin nodded. "I was surprised to hear that you're headed back to Texas."

"That's the plan." Grady glanced at Gina standing on the deck. It was tempting to stay, but a bad choice. "I'm only here until my grandfather is able to care for himself."

Hilliard let out a sigh. "I was hoping you'd think about training your dogs here."

Grady wonder what the man's point would be. "Why is that?"

"A couple of reasons. I run an extreme ski resort. People pay a hefty price to get the thrill of pushing it to the limit on the mountaintop. With that, there's always a threat of a possible avalanche. You know how critical time is in finding a buried skier and the mountain rescue squad here is one of the best. Call me a control freak if you will, but I like to have my own resources. My own qualified rescue team that I could airlift at a moment's notice."

Grady was surprised. "You want your own rescue dogs?"

Justin nodded. "Not just dogs, but I want a team with their handlers. And I'll pay well for it."

"Just for the winter?"

"Colorado has a long ski season." Hilliard went on to say, "I'm also developing mountain bike trails, with a training facility that will open in a few months. People go off the trail and get lost, even experienced hikers and bikers. I'd like to offer them that sense of security, especially since I'll be responsible for a lot of amateurs not used to the rough terrain."

Grady didn't want to be interested in the project, but he was. "You have a lot going on."

Justin nodded. "I do. I like living in a small town the size of Destiny. It's a great place to raise a family. Tourism is our main economy here." He glanced around. "This is all too beautiful to change. A lot of opportunity for someone with your talent." He handed him a business card. "If you have a chance, stop by my office at the Heritage Mountain Complex, and I'll show you my biking trails."

Grady took the card. "I can't promise anything."

"I understand, but I'd like a chance to show you what I could offer you and your partner."

Before Grady could say any more, Zack raced up to him. "Grady, look, Bandit found this." He waved the old T-shirt, but he held on to the leash with his other hand. "I buried it, and Josh took him out to search and he found it."

Justin excused himself and walked away.

Grady knelt and petted the boy's dog. "Hey, that's a good start."

The kids agreed. "And I want to train him more," Zack told him.

"It not something that's going to happen overnight, son. Scout took months and he was worked with every day."

"If you show me what to do, I'll work with Bandit every day. I promise. And my mom can bring Bandit out to you on the weekends so he can let Scout show him what to do, too."

That was the last thing Grady needed, more time with Gina. "Why don't you concentrate on Bandit being a good friend? You don't need him to be a rescue dog."

He saw the disappointment on the boy's face. Suddenly the memory of being a neglected kid with no one having time for him rushed back. "Okay, how about this?" Grady said. "What if I bring Scout into town a couple of afternoons and we'll spend time teaching Bandit a simple command?"

The boy's eyes rounded. "Really?"

"Zack, I'm willing to help, but I'm not going to be around very much longer."

The kid looked shocked and sad. "Why? Aren't you going to live in the cabin and train rescue dogs?"

"I'm only training here temporarily. I'll be going home to Texas." He hadn't had a home anywhere in a long time. "As soon as my granddad is better."

The boy's eyes lit up. "What if he doesn't get better for a long time? Can you still help me with Bandit?"

He found he would miss the boy, too. "Only if it's okay with your mother."

"If what's okay with me?"

Grady turned around to find Gina approaching them. He felt his mouth go dry, hating that she had that effect on him.

"Mom, Grady said he'll help me train Bandit. Please, can he?"

"Zack. We talked about this. You can't take up all Grady's time. He needs to work with his dogs, too."

Grady stepped in. "I wouldn't have offered if I didn't want to do it."

She didn't look convinced. "Zack… Why don't you go and get Bandit some water?"

Once the boy and dog were gone, she spoke. "Grady, you don't have to do this."

The sound of her saying his name did things to him. "It's really not a problem."

It was a problem for Gina. She didn't need to spend any more time with this man. "Still, your time is valuable."

"So is yours and you took the time to straighten up the cabin. Speaking of which, I need to ask you a favor."

What could he possibly need from her? "Sure. Whatever you need."

"My grandfather wants to talk to you about the furniture."

"Does he want it all back?" she asked. "Of course he does. I haven't sold any of it, so the sofas can go back."

She looked up to catch him smiling. "What?"

"You can't let Fletch intimidate you. That cabin was a disgrace. It's needed to be cleaned out for years. I only want you to check with him about a few of my grandmother's things."

"Of course. I'm sure you want them to stay in the family, something to hand down to the next generation."

He frowned. "That's something that isn't going to happen. The Fletcher line ends with me."

Gina watched as Grady walked off to care for the dogs. Okay, she'd said the wrong things again. Did he think he wouldn't ever marry, ever have children?

"Hey, sis," Lori called to her.

They hugged. "Hi, Lori. Glad you could make it." She glanced at her niece, Cassie, who was already playing with the others.

"Jace had a business call." Lori looked at the group with the dogs. "Seems you got here early enough to spend time with the popular dog trainer."

"Don't get any ideas," she warned. "It was Zack who wanted to bring Bandit. Besides, I'm doing business with Grady. He's cleaning out his grandfather's cabin and the furniture is filling up the shop."

"He's also a man who spends time with your child. I'd say that's a good quality. I take it he's going to help Zack train Bandit."

"I don't know, Lori. Why don't you ask him?"

Her sister looked taken aback by her attitude. "Are you okay?"

She released a breath. "Yes. Sorry, I'm just tired of everyone asking me about Grady. Don't get me wrong.

I'm so grateful the man found Zack, but that's as far as it goes. He's not my man. We're not together in any way." She took a shaky breath, unable to stop the awful memories from her marriage. "I'm not ready to be with a man, Lori.... I might never be."

"Shh. It's okay, Gina." Lori took her hand and walked away from the group for more privacy. "I'm sorry I said anything. And I promise I won't push you anymore. But be assured, when you find that right man, you'll be able to trust again."

Gina felt that familiar lonely ache that tore at her. She glanced at the good-looking ex-sergeant and a different kind of feeling washed over her.

She quickly averted her eyes away from temptation. "What if I'm never ready, Lori? What if I can't stand to ever let a man touch me again?"

She studied her. "Are you still going to your support group?"

"As much as I can. I've been focused on Zack lately."

"You need to focus on yourself, too." She smiled. "Who knows, you might start feeling secure enough you'd trust a nice man like Grady Fletcher."

Gina started to argue and her sister stopped her by saying, "Just don't rule the man out."

Gina knew she couldn't risk it. Besides, the man wouldn't be here long enough. He was headed back to Texas and out of her life.

Two mornings later Grady pulled up behind the Second Best Thrift Shop and parked. Maybe he should have called Gina first, but it had all been a bit last-minute. Then he'd got the call from Shady Haven. His grandfather had summoned him.

He might as well get this over with so he could get

back to work at the cabin. He climbed out of the truck and headed for the large back door. He opened it and peered inside. Marie was in the work area, stretching fabric over the arm of one of the sofas he'd given to Gina.

She saw him right away and stood. "Hello, Grady. What brings you here? You find more treasures?"

"What you call treasures, I call junk." He glanced around. "Is Gina here?"

Just then the woman in question walked through the door from the front showroom. She was dressed in her standard dark slacks, but today she had on a soft white-and-navy-striped blouse. It was fitted, showing off her narrow waist and nice curves. Her long dark hair was pulled back into a ponytail and hoop earrings hung from her ears.

She finally spotted him. "Oh, hi, Grady. What are you doing in town?"

He found he could easily get lost in her green eyes. "Ah, I got a call from my grandfather. He was wondering if you had time to see him today."

"I'm not sure…"

"I told him he couldn't order people around just to please himself."

Marie stood. "Gina, I can watch the shop. Sophie is here, so it's fine for me to stay."

Gina checked her watch. "Okay, but I'll have a sandwich sent over from the Silver Spoon. My treat."

"No, it'll be my treat," Grady insisted. "We'll take Fletch a piece of pie, too."

Gina couldn't think of any more excuses not to go. She went to get her purse and realized her heart was beating like a drum, hard and fast. She had to pull herself together and stop letting him get to her.

She followed him to the truck and let him help her in, and that meant he touched her. Oh, God. She felt his heat and his strength as he lifted her up into the vehicle. Once fastened in, she laid her head back and tried to relax. Grady didn't seem to be any more talkative than she. Thank goodness the trip to the restaurant was quick, then the ride outside of town only took about fifteen minutes.

Grady finally broke the silence when he announced, "We're here."

He parked in the Shady Haven lot, then they walked up to the entrance of the two-story building. "Just one thing before we go in. Don't let my grandfather get to you. He thinks because he's old he can say and do whatever he wants. If he gets too personal, tell him to back off."

"I'm sure he'll be perfectly nice," she said.

Grady wasn't sure what Joe Fletcher wanted with Gina. He figured it was because he hadn't been out for a few days, and the man was probably lonely.

They walked through the double doors of the facility. "Oh, Grady, it's lovely here."

He had to agree. "I tried to tell Fletch that he'd be more comfortable moving in here, but he misses the cabin." He went to the desk and asked the receptionist for his grandfather.

The young woman sent them into the recreation room. Grady guided her down the hall to a large area that had a huge flat-screen television. The walls were lined with bookshelves filled with books. There seemed to be a lot of activities going on, and a lot of interaction between the patients and other guests.

There were several small tables for games. That's

where he found his grandfather with three women. They were playing cards.

"There he is." He put his hand against Gina's back and guided her through the room.

"Well, well, Granddad," Grady said as he stopped at the card table. "Seems you're not so lonely anymore."

Joe Fletcher glared at him. "It's a shame I need to call you to come and see me."

"I was here two days ago."

"Oh, Joe, is this your grandson?" asked one of the gray-haired women at the table. "He's just as handsome as you said."

"Grady, meet Alice, Mary Lou and Bubbles."

He nodded as they seemed to be blushing at his attention. "Ladies and Granddad, this is Gina Williams."

She stepped forward. "It's nice to meet everyone." She looked at Joe. "And especially you, Mr. Fletcher."

Joe Fletcher smiled as he looked Gina over. "Well, well, you're mighty pretty, Miss Williams. I can see why my grandson has been distracted lately."

"Granddad," Grady said in warning.

Gina blushed. "Why, thank you, Mr. Fletcher, but I think Grady's been busy with training his dogs."

"That's probably true. Sad, but true," Joe said, then excused himself from the ladies at the table. Grady took charge of Fletch's wheelchair and they crossed the room to an empty table.

"Can't wait to get out of this contraption." Joe hit the arm of the wheelchair. "I can't even go to the bathroom by myself."

Grady sat. "Fletch, you know once you finish rehab, you'll be able to walk again. All the doctors said so."

"I could be dead by then."

Gina sat across from the older man. "Mr. Fletcher,

you should listen to your grandson. He's been trying to make the cabin ready for your return, but you have to do your part."

Grady bit back a grin.

Fletch finally smiled. "I like you, Gina Williams. Besides being pretty as a new spotted pup, you seem to have a head on your shoulders."

"Sometimes we learn from our mistakes." She handed him the container with the pie. "Here, Grady brought this for you."

He took the offered dessert. "Do you have a man in your life?"

Gina wasn't going to fall into this trap. "Yes, I do, as a matter of fact. And I love him to death. In fact, he and Grady are very good friends."

The thin man raised a bushy gray eyebrow. "Then he must be a good guy if Grady likes him."

"Of course. Grady even got him a dog, Bandit, and is going to help train him. Of course, we both got worried when the dog took off and followed Zack to school."

"School?" Joe wasn't dumb by any means. "Just how old is this man?"

"He's nearly eight." She glanced at Grady and felt a rush of admiration, something she didn't want to admit. "Your Grady and Scout saved my son's life." She swallowed back the emotion. "I will always be grateful."

Fletch smiled. "So it was your boy who got lost?"

"Yes. That's why I want to help to fix up the cabin. You had a lot of furniture, Mr. Fletcher. But if there's a question about anything I have in my store, of course I will return it."

The old man shrugged. "There's not much I care to save. My wife had a bunch of frilly stuff—" he glanced at Grady "—I'm sure my grandson could care less about."

Gina asked, "Is there anything you care about, Mr. Fletcher?"

He gave her a big grin. "Just my bed. I love my big brass bed."

She smiled. "Oh, I've seen it. It's lovely."

"Glad you like it. Someday Grady is going to inherit that bed."

An hour later, filled with several long stories of the past, Grady and Gina said goodbye to Fletch and walked out of Shady Haven.

Gina was quiet as she thought about Grady and his grandfather reminiscing about their past summers together. She got a sneak peak of a side to Grady she hadn't seen before, a more relaxed, a more outgoing side. She doubted that Grady had revealed it to many, and she felt lucky to get a glimpse of this man.

What she quickly discovered was that she'd like to know more about Grady. Spend more time with him, find out if he wanted more from her than just a spontaneous kiss in the garage.

She glanced at the handsome man beside her. There was a sudden tingling in her stomach, something she hadn't felt in a long time.

Was Lori right? Maybe she was ready to move on.

They reached the truck and Grady turned to her and said, "I'm sorry Fletch bored you going on and on with those stories, and the questions. You should have told him to mind his own business."

Gina smiled up at him. "Fletch is a wonderful old man. And you're pretty wonderful, too."

Grady didn't have time to react as Gina rose up,

locked her hands around his neck, pulled him down and covered his mouth with a kiss. Caught off balance, he gripped the sides of her waist and just managed to hold on. As kisses went, what she lacked in experience, she made up for in enthusiasm. He could get into this. Then she quickly released him, looking shocked at her actions.

"Not that I'm complaining, but didn't I just get into trouble for doing the same thing last week?"

Her cheeks were rosy with embarrassment. "You act so big and tough. Then I see how sweet you are with kids…and how much you care for your grandfather."

He leaned against the truck and couldn't help but smile. This woman was so appealing, and so much trouble. That meant he should stay far away from her.

"Hell, if I'd known that would earn me a kiss from you, I'd have brought you here to see Fletch sooner."

"Oh, maybe I shouldn't have done that." Her face flamed even more and her gaze darted away.

He touched her chin and made her look at him. "Did you hear me complain?"

She only shook her head.

He wanted nothing more than to continue kissing her, but knew better than to go any further. That still didn't stop him from asking, "How would you like to get some lunch?"

She looked surprised at his offer. "I shouldn't. I mean, Marie is already staying later." She hesitated. "I guess I could call her."

He pulled out his phone. "What's the number?"

CHAPTER NINE

TWENTY minutes later Grady escorted Gina into the Silver Spoon Restaurant. They walked through the glass-paneled door and were greeted by a surprised Helen Turner. The middle-aged owner was wearing jeans and a white blouse, covered by a starched apron. She also had on a big smile.

"Well, well, isn't this nice." She set down two glasses of water as they slid into a booth in front of the window. "Twice in one day."

Grady spoke up. "We took the pie out to my grand-dad and realized we hadn't eaten."

"How is Joe?" Helen asked. "Did he enjoy the pie?"

"Yes, he did. He told me to tell you it was delicious."

Helen grinned. "Well if that just doesn't make my day." She handed out the menus. "I may have to go see that old man."

After the woman walked off, Grady leaned forward. "No doubt by tonight the town will be buzzing about us being together." He looked around the room, seeing glances from the curious patrons. "They're probably wondering what an old guy like me is doing with someone as pretty as you."

"You aren't old, and thank you for saying I'm pretty."

He leaned back in the booth. "He sure did a job on you, didn't he?"

Gina didn't want to talk about her past, or her ex. "It's not something I'm proud of."

Grady wanted to set her straight, but Helen reappeared and took their order. After she left he said, "That's what you have to change, Gina. Your way of thinking that anything that bastard did was your fault." He leaned closer again, his eyes locked on hers as his voice lowered. "It wasn't, Gina. You found the courage to take your son and leave him. I'd say you're a pretty amazing woman."

Gina's heart was pounding at Grady's words. "Thank you."

"I'm speaking the truth. You're making a fresh start for yourself and Zack. You're building a business that seems to be doing well. Soon there'll be men lining up to spend time with you."

She quickly shook her head. She couldn't stop the panic she felt building up inside. "I'm not sure I can get involved with a man again."

"Why not? You managed to kiss me."

She didn't want to rehash her sudden impulsiveness. It had been so unlike her. "You're different."

He frowned. "I don't know if I like the sound of that."

She shrugged. "I've got to know you. I trust you." And she was attracted to him, she added silently. "Too bad I can't practice on you."

Grady hadn't been surprised after Gina's admission that lunch was eaten quickly and the subject had been changed to work. Twenty minutes later Grady drove Gina back to her store. He parked out back and she thanked him, then couldn't get out of the truck fast enough.

He sat there a few minutes, telling himself what Gina had said at the Silver Spoon was just joking around. He needed to let it go. So why couldn't he?

Grady climbed out of the driver's side and walked to the back door of the store. He said hi to Marie as she pushed a baby stroller out the door.

He moved into the work area and stopped, amazed to see that the old sofas were nearly finished. One was covered in a gray-and-white stripe, and the other was in a camel color. He smiled as he imagined all the work Gina and Marie had put into them.

He went down a hall past an office, then a small bathroom. He continued his journey into the main room where there was furniture arranged in groups. Against the far wall were lamps and several dining room tables and chairs. He moved toward the front and discovered a high counter. Gina stood behind it with her back to him, talking on the phone.

"Yes, Mrs. Browning, I can be out tomorrow morning." She paused. "Of course, I'll give you my price before I take anything. Okay, goodbye." She hung up and turned around.

That was when she saw him. "Grady. I thought you left."

He should have. He was crazy to be here to pursue any part of this woman. "What did you mean by saying you want to practice on me?"

Gina groaned. She was so embarrassed. "Oh, that. I was just kidding around."

He came behind the desk. "Were you joking around when you planted that kiss on me at Shady Haven?"

He wasn't going to let this go, she realized. "Gosh,

you caught me. I was impulsive and talkative all in one day." She waved him off. "Just forget it happened."

He moved closer as he pushed his cowboy hat back off his forehead. "What if I don't want to forget it? What if I want to hear what you're thinking?"

Gina brushed back her hair, feeling her heart racing with him standing so close. "You've got to have better things to do than—"

"Than what?" he asked. "Show you how to kiss properly? How to feel comfortable around a man?"

She swallowed. Her throat was bone-dry. "It sounds silly to hear you say it. Besides I don't have time to date anyway. Zack needs my attention." She sighed, trying to push away the endless loneliness she always felt. "But there are times when I don't want to be alone."

"Like in the middle of the night?"

She wasn't ready to admit that yet. "More like when you get invited places and you're the fifth wheel, or everyone wants to fix you up with someone. I'm tired of the pity. The poor girl whose husband was abusive… the poor girl who had it so rough."

He reached out and touched her cheek. "First of all, you aren't a girl anymore, Gina. You're definitely a woman. A strong woman who has started a new life and is doing a good job of raising her son. Those who think differently, to hell with them."

He lowered his head and her heart began to race. "Now, as for the amount of instruction you'll need, first I'll need to sample you again."

Before she could say anything, his mouth closed over hers. It was soft, a whisper of a kiss, teasing her, making her want more.

Before she could react, Grady pulled back a little, enough for her to see his dark gaze. "Open just a little,

Gina." It wasn't a demand, but a request as his thumb caressed her lower lip. "Perfect," he breathed, then went back for more. This time he added some pressure, then his hands went to her face and held her tenderly. His mouth moved over hers, tasting and caressing until she lost all track of everything except this man. *Oh, my,* she sighed in a moan as her hands came up to his chest. His tongue teased along the seam of her lips, then darted inside when she opened wider. And her own body's reaction caused an ache she'd never felt before.

He pulled back and looked down at her. She couldn't miss the desire she saw in his eyes.

She managed to speak. "How was I?"

"I think you know the answer already. I want you, Gina." He released a breath. "Does that frighten you?"

She was thrilled at his declaration, but scared to death. But knowing how much she wanted to move on, to take a chance on finding happiness. "Yes! No! I don't know, but I do trust you."

Those words seemed to bring him back to reality. He took a step back. "Don't make that mistake. You need to find a man who wants to settle down and have a family. Someone closer to your age."

She didn't remove her hands from Grady's chest. She didn't want to break the contact with him. "You have this thing about your age. You're not that much older than I am." She moved closer to him. "It didn't feel like an old man kissing me."

"You're asking for trouble."

She raised an eyebrow, going after what she wanted. To stop letting the past dictate the future. "Seems you are, too. Isn't that the reason you walked in here?"

She saw the confusion in his eyes. She forced herself to stand her ground.

"I need to go," he said, and she was a little relieved and a little disappointed when Grady turned and walked out.

It was Tuesday and Grady had promised Zack that he'd work with him after school. Since he'd walked out of Second Best four days ago he hadn't contacted Gina. He hadn't even called her, and that was for the best.

He needed time to think, needed to come to his senses. It hadn't done any good, though. The bottom line was he wanted to be with Gina Williams. And yet, he wanted more than just to spend time with her. He wanted to get her naked, to make love to her until they both couldn't think about anything else.

He released a breath. He hadn't been with any woman since his divorce. And not since he'd been burned. He touched the scar above his shirt collar and recalled Gina's hands on his chest. A portion of his upper body had been burned, too. Would the scar repulse her?

He turned down Cherry Street and found Zack was waiting for him at the curb as he got out of the vehicle.

"Hi, Grady. I've been working with Bandit every day. He's been behaving really well, too."

He retrieved Scout from the back. "Glad to hear it. Let's go see how he works today."

Grady placed his hand on the boy's shoulder as they headed to the side gate and into the backyard. Gina came out of the sliding door off the deck. He stopped cold seeing her in snug jeans and a T-shirt. Her legs might not be that long, but they were toned and shapely. Her hair was pulled back into a ponytail.

She smiled. "Hi, Grady."

"Gina."

She came down the steps and he had to stop himself

from reaching for her and giving her the proper greeting he'd been aching to do since he'd left her four long days ago.

"How have you been?" he asked.

"Good." She beamed and her eyes brightened. "I sold the camelback sofa today." She giggled. "I got six hundred dollars for it."

He blinked. "Hey, that's a good profit."

"I'm glad I could give Marie a nice bonus, too. She and her husband could use the money. I feel like I should give you some, too."

He shook his head. "You did me a favor and hauled it out. I should have paid you."

"Okay, we'll call it even."

Zack came up to him. "Grady, can we start now?"

Okay, so now she was distracting him from his job. "Sure."

He walked off with Zack and for the next hour they worked Scout, all the time hoping that Bandit would follow the boy's commands, too.

Grady observed the boy and his dog. He was impressed at how well the kid handled the large animal. "Okay, tell Bandit to heel."

Zack had his dog on the leash at his left side. The twosome began walking, then Zack gave the command and Bandit obeyed. Both dogs were rewarded with some play time. They tossed tennis balls so the animals could retrieve them.

Zack came up to him. "Grady, can I ask you a question?"

He was surprised the see the serious look on the boy's face. "Sure, I'm not guaranteeing I'll have an answer."

"Does the scar on your neck hurt?"

Grady knelt and the animals came up to him. He had them sit and gave his full attention to the boy. "It used to hurt a lot," he answered honestly. "Not so much anymore."

"Did you get it when you were fighting the bad guys?"

He wasn't sure he could explain it to a seven-year-old. "Yes. There are a lot of us over there fighting."

"My teacher says you're making it safe for all of us so we can live free. And we should always thank you."

Grady nodded. "There were many soldiers who gave their lives for that freedom, too." He couldn't help but think of the men he'd lost that day. "Honor them for their sacrifice."

"I will," Zack promised. "I'm glad you came home, Grady. Really glad."

Zack smiled. "I'm glad you live in Destiny, too."

Before Grady could contradict the boy, Gina called out, "Supper's ready."

Grady glanced up, not surprised to see her curious look. He stood. "I've got to be going."

"No, please stay," Gina coaxed. "Unless you have plans."

He could lie, but Josh had gone out tonight, so he was just going to pick up a sandwich in town before heading back to the cabin. "No plans."

She smiled. "Good. I hope you like meat loaf."

What does one meal hurt? "You're talking to a man who spent twenty years in the military. We appreciate any home cooking we can get."

Leaving Scout out on the deck with Bandit, he walked into the homey kitchen. Not the most updated appliances, and the countertops were chipped, but Gina had painted the walls a soft green and added those womanly touches.

"We've got to wash up," Zack said, and took him down the hall. There was a detour into the kid's bedroom. It was blue with a lot of baseball posters on the walls.

Grady said, "I guess you like the game."

"I get to play Little League next month, but I'm not very good. Uncle Jace has been practicing with me, but I still have trouble catching."

"You'll get better with practice."

"But the other boys have been playing for two years." Zack moved his gaze away. "I didn't get to play when I lived with my dad. He didn't like me playing 'cause I couldn't do anything right."

Grady knelt down to be eye level with the sad boy. He worked to hide the anger he felt toward Lowell. "You have to know that your dad didn't treat you right. It had nothing to do with you. None of it was your fault. You can do anything you want to do. Look how much you've accomplished with Bandit."

The boy's head bobbed up and down. "And now Mommy and me don't have to be scared. I'm glad my dad went away."

So was Grady. "And he's never going to hurt either you or your mom again. Sheriff Larkin will make sure of that."

Zack threw his arms around Grady's neck. "Thanks, Grady. And I'm glad you're around, too."

There was a sudden constriction in his chest as he felt those tiny arms around him. He couldn't help but wonder if his son had survived, how close they would have been. Would they have had moments like this?

"You're welcome, kid." He stood.

After washing their hands, they went back into the hall and walked past another bedroom. No doubt it was Gina's. The walls were painted a soft yellow. It had a queen-size bed with a solid pale blue comforter, adorned with several pillows. As much as he tried to fight it, he could picture her in that big bed, with all that pretty dark hair spread out on the pillow.

He blinked away the daydream and caught up with Zack as they entered the kitchen where the food was on the table. Zack took his seat, then Gina sat. An ache filled him as he took the empty seat.

Okay, maybe he did want this. As a kid, he'd never been part of a family. The army had been the family he'd shared his life with. He looked at Gina. Why now? What was it about her that made him want something he'd already failed at miserably?

Two hours later Gina was surprised that Grady was still there. He'd insisted that he and Zack would do the dishes, then the next thing she knew, he was helping her son with his homework.

Once Zack was tucked into bed, she went in and kissed her son good-night. When she came back out to the living room she found Grady waiting by the front door, hat in hand.

"I've got to go."

She nodded. "Of course. I'm sorry, I didn't mean to take up so much of your evening."

He reached for the doorknob and stopped. "I'm not good at this, Gina. I've tried before and I made a lot of mistakes."

He must be talking about his marriage.

"I didn't mean to bring back bad memories. I'm sorry, Grady." She glanced away, feeling foolish about all those kisses they'd shared the other day. "Thank you for all your help with Zack."

She heard his curse, then he reached for her. She gasped, not from fear, but from surprise when his mouth closed over hers. She was hungry for him, praying all evening that he'd kiss her again.

He broke off the kiss. "Damn. I shouldn't have done that." His dark brooding gaze searched her face. "It's not you, Gina."

That made her angry. "Even I have heard that line before. If you don't want to get involved with me, that's okay, but don't make up excuses."

"Dammit, I'm not a good bet." He glanced around. "My marriage was a disaster."

She wasn't sure if she wanted to know that he had loved another woman. "How long were you married?"

"Five years." He laughed. "On paper, but in reality, we weren't together much of that time. I was overseas twice. The second time was the clincher. Barbara left me."

"I'm sorry, Grady. I know that must have hurt you."

"Not as badly as I hurt her. I was never there for her. I can't blame her for ending it."

"If you were in the army when you got married, she had to know that you'd be away a lot."

"That's easier said than done. Barb asked me not to go, but I chose a unit that was going to be deployed. I chose 'the cause' over her." His pained gaze met hers. "I realized then that I could never be a permanent kind of guy. And that's exactly the type you and Zack need, a family man."

She nodded, understanding what he was trying to tell her. "Someday I want to give my son the security of a family." She hesitated, feeling her fears and emotion surface. "That's what I'm afraid of, Grady, that I never will be able to. I'd been with Eric since I was a teenager. He's been the only man I've…known. I'd never even kissed another man until you."

Grady was shocked at her confession. "Hell, Gina, there's a hell of a lot of men out there who would love the chance."

She stepped away, and he missed her closeness. "I lost so much of my adolescence, and with my abusive marriage, I'm frightened to try another relationship." Her rich green eyes met his. "I don't know if I can ever be with a man again." Her voice lowered to a whisper. "Not intimately anyway."

He fought going to her and proving her wrong. "It'll take time, but I'm sure you'll find someone."

He watched her swallow, square her shoulders, then she asked, "Would you help me, Grady?"

Not what he expected her to say. Of course nothing had been what he'd expected since he'd met this woman. Common sense told him to leave, but that didn't stop his ache for her. His head said to run away. He didn't want to know what his heart said.

"That's the worst idea I ever heard."

"Why? I trust you."

"That's your first mistake. You shouldn't." He started to pace. "You don't want a man who will take what he wants from you then leave. And I am leaving, Gina. As soon as Fletch is well enough, I'm gone."

She nodded. "I know. That's what makes this work. You can show me how a man is supposed to treat a woman, and when it comes time for you to leave, I won't try and stop you."

"It isn't always a clean break. You could get hurt."

"I'll be sad when you leave, but if I know that it's

coming, I can deal with it." She walked toward him. "I just want to know what it's like to be in a normal, healthy relationship. One where I get to be an equal partner. One where a man doesn't control me, make me do things that I don't want to do."

She blinked and glanced away. He went to her and turned her face toward him. He saw the pain and hurt. He wanted to erase all of it.

"Hey. Shh." He bent down and brushed his mouth over hers, once, then twice, listening to her soft moans of wanting.

"You said the other day you wanted me," she said. "Have you changed your mind?"

He answered as his mouth captured hers in a hungry kiss. He drew her close, careful not to be too rough. He pressed her body against his, letting her feel his desire. "Does that answer your question?"

She was breathing hard. "Oh, yes. I want you, too, Grady Fletcher."

CHAPTER TEN

HE WAS nothing but a coward.

Later the next morning Grady pulled into Shady Haven's parking lot, unable to forget how twelve hours ago, he'd run out on Gina. Facing the enemy in a foreign country had been easier than dealing with this 110-pound woman.

All night Gina had invaded his sleep, along with his peace of mind. Any rational thinking on his part had disappeared because he was actually considering her crazy idea.

Worse, it was affecting his concentration with the dogs this morning. Even Josh had noticed he'd been distracted. Finally, Grady had ended the struggle and decided to go visit his grandfather. But if the old guy brought up Gina Williams, he wasn't going to be held responsible for his actions.

Grady walked inside and the receptionist looked up and smiled, then she pointed toward the recreation room. There was no doubt his grandfather was the social one in the family. Grady headed down the hall and found Fletch sitting at his usual table with a younger woman. Lori Hutchinson Yeager.

What was she doing here?

He walked over and his grandfather smiled at him. "Hey, son, I didn't expect to see you this morning."

"Here I thought you might be lonely. I'm glad to see you're not." Grady turned his attention to Gina's pretty blond sister. "Hello, Lori."

She nodded. "Hi, Grady. I didn't mean to take up all your grandfather's time. It was important that I clear up something with Joe." She smiled at his grandfather. "We've just finished with our business."

Grady sat and asked, "And exactly what business would that be?"

His grandfather spoke up. "Watch your manners, son. Miss Lori is nice enough to come out here and correct a grave mistake she found." He nodded to Lori. "Tell my grandson, Miss Lori."

"Of course," Lori said. "Grady, I can understand your concern, but this is good. I mentioned something to you a few weeks ago about a questionable parcel of land of my great-grandfather Billy had the papers for. We discovered that he didn't really own it, at least not legally. He took it from your grandfather saying he hadn't paid the taxes. Since I took over running the bank this past year, I discovered the taxes assessed on the property were three times the normal rate." She sighed. "I'm not proud of what Billy did. So I hope after today, I've corrected the issue about the land. It will be returned to Joe."

Grady wasn't sure what was going on. "Fletch doesn't need another old abandoned mine."

"That's what is great about this, Grady," Fletch began, "It isn't a worthless mine. It's prime land just outside of Destiny. It belonged to your grandmother and now, thanks to Miss Lori, we have it back." His grandfather grinned. "And I'm going to deed it over to you."

Grady was skeptical of all this, but the look on his grandfather's face was priceless.

Lori smiled. "Well, I should get back to the bank. If

it's all right with you, I'll have Paige Larkin start the paperwork."

Joe looked at his grandson. Grady nodded.

"Okay, then," Lori said. "In a few days the papers will be ready to sign."

She stood and so did Grady. That was when he noticed the roundness of her stomach. Gina's sister was expecting? "I'll walk you out," he offered.

"I'll be right back," he told Fletch, then he escorted Lori down the hall.

"I hope you'll accept my apology for the actions of my great-grandfather," Lori said. "As I told your grandfather, I've been trying to correct a lot of Billy's mistakes. Thank goodness, I'm nearly at the end of the list."

"I appreciate your efforts," Grady told her. "You've made Fletch happy. He needs something to look forward to."

Lori stopped at the building entry. "I'm glad." She hesitated. "I can't thank you for all the help you've given to my sister and nephew."

"Not a problem."

"It's still nice that you've been helping Zack with Bandit."

"And if I want to spend time with Zack's mother?"

That brought a smile to her lovely face, reminding him of Gina. "You don't strike me as the type of man who asks for permission."

Maybe he'd changed. "How about if I ask if you'll watch Zack one evening?"

"Of course I would." She grinned and headed to the door, then looked back. "He loves to sleep over at Aunt Lori's house."

* * *

It was a date. She had a date with Grady.

That was all, Gina told herself as she kept changing her outfit. She didn't exactly have many choices of what to wear.

"Here, put on these," Lori offered. She held up a pair of expensive jeans. "They'll look great with your teal sweater."

"I can't wear your pants. What if I spill something on them?"

"Come on, sis. They're a pair of jeans. I'll buy more after the baby comes." She rubbed her bottom. "That is if I ever lose the weight."

"You look great. And more importantly, your loving husband thinks so."

She held out the pair of denims to her. "Then wear them."

Gina relented and stepped into the jeans. Thank goodness the fabric had stretch in it, or she would never get them zipped. She turned from side to side to get a look. Not bad. She slipped on the sweater and put on another loan from sis, a pair of high-heeled sandals. She stood. Okay, she looked taller. What would Grady think?

Just then the doorbell sounded and her heart began to pound. "Oh, he's here."

"Slow down," her sister coaxed. "It won't hurt him to wait a few minutes. You're worth it."

Gina agreed, knowing she had to reprogram her way of thinking. From now on men were going to treat her right.

After applying lipstick, she grabbed her purse and walked out to the living room to find Grady talking with Zack.

Oh, my. He looked so…wonderful. Dressed in a burgundy Western shirt that was fitted over those broad shoulders and tucked neatly into a pair of killer black jeans.

Her son turned around. "Oh, Mom," he called. "You look so pretty."

"Thank you, Zack." She felt the heat rush to her face as she glanced at Grady. "Hello, Grady."

"Hi, Gina." His gaze was dark and intense, then he smiled as he made his way to her. "Your son's right, you do look pretty."

More heat shot to her face. "Thank you."

She managed to kiss her son goodbye before he walked out the front door with Aunt Lori.

The room grew silent as Grady stood at the closed door, his gaze moving over her body. "What you do to a pair of jeans should be outlawed."

She found she was a little breathless. "You should be happy. I can't eat much in these."

He walked to her, leaned down and brushed a soft kiss against her lips. "We'd better get out of here, or I might just decide to skip food all together."

She swallowed. "Oh, no you don't, Grady Fletcher, you promised me dinner." She grabbed his hand and hauled him toward the door and they laughed all the way to the truck.

The trip to Durango took about forty minutes. It wasn't that Grady didn't want to take Gina to dinner in Destiny. He just didn't want everyone watching them, speculating on their relationship. What they were doing or not doing was no one's business.

Damn. What was he doing? He was too old to start the dating game.

Grady parked in the public lot and escorted Gina the

two blocks to Main Street and Francisco's Restaurant. Although he'd made a reservation, he took her into the bar and sat. "Would you like something to drink?"

At first she turned him down, but when the waitress suggested their famous margarita, Gina agreed to try it. Once the large glass arrived, she looked intimidated, but took a sip. "This is good."

Grady took a drink of his beer. "Just be careful. Tequila has been known to sneak up on you."

"Are you talking from experience?"

He couldn't help but smile. "Could be. In my younger and not-so-wiser days."

"I never had the chance to do much of anything. I got married when I was barely out of high school. I never went out much, or had girlfriends." She took another sip, then said, "I guess I'm overdue some experience…life."

They exchanged a glance that told him she wasn't talking just about the alcohol and his gut tightened. There was so much he wanted to share with this woman.

Finally the waitress took them to their table in a quiet corner. It was next to the fireplace and the sound of soft music filled the room. Gina sat at an angle to him. He found he liked her close, close enough to touch.

"This is lovely, Grady," she said. "Thank you for bringing me here."

It was hard to believe that she'd never been taken out to a nice meal. "You're welcome." He had to stop thinking about all the "firsts" he wanted to share with her. The waitress handed them menus and Grady opened his. "I hear the seafood is good."

Gina started to look hers over. "Oh, there's so much. Will you order for me?" she asked.

He shook his head. "Tonight, Gina, you're making your own choices."

She looked at him, her green eyes leery. She glanced over the list again. "Well, then, I'm going to have…the penne pasta and scallops." She closed the menu and handed it to the waitress.

"I'm a pretty basic meat-and-potatoes kind of guy. I'll have the rib-eye steak, medium rare."

The waitress smiled then walked away.

Gina liked that she wasn't nervous with Grady. Maybe it was the margarita that helped her relax, but she found herself at ease with him. "There's nothing basic about you, Sarge."

He gave her a stern look, then his expression softened. He reached for her hand. "I'm sure you're going to tell me why you think that."

She took another sip of her drink and said, "Maybe later. I don't think I need to inflate your ego any more."

"Wait a minute. I have an inflated ego?"

She laughed. "I was teasing. It's that you've accomplished so many things, and you've probably done everything very well."

He took a drink of his beer. "You just don't know my failures."

She studied his handsome face. "There can't be many. You had a long career in the army. I can see the respect you get from Josh. I suspect all the men in your unit felt the same about you."

It was endearing to see him blush. "Aren't you the wise one?"

Gina felt the warmth of his hand caressing hers. It sent shivers up her arm, making her aware that she was female. She glanced away and took a breath for courage before she turned back to him. She caught his gaze on her. The things this man could do to her with only a look.

She sobered. "I know a lot has changed with your accident and retiring from the military… But, Grady, you've already started a new career that you love. I'd say, all in all, you're a pretty lucky guy."

Grady didn't want to get into his past or his future. This was only about tonight. He squeezed her hand. "I feel lucky that I'm with the prettiest woman here."

She smiled at him and his gut tightened. "Thank you for saying that."

"Someone should be telling you that all the time." He just couldn't be that guy, he added silently. "You're special, Gina."

"I guess we should start each other's fan clubs." She giggled and he found he liked the sound. That was the problem. He liked too many things about this woman.

About two hours later Grady pulled up in front of her house. He turned off the engine and sat back wondering what was going to happen next. He knew he didn't want the evening to end, but it also wouldn't be wise to stay. No matter how much he wanted Gina, he wouldn't take advantage of her. If he did take things further, it wouldn't change anything between them. In the end, he'd be leaving town.

He walked around the truck, opened the passenger-side door and helped Gina out. They made their way along the walkway and up the steps. She put the key into the lock and opened the door.

She turned back to him. "Would you like to come in for some coffee?"

With any other woman that would be a signal for something else, but with Gina, she was most likely going to fix him coffee. "Sure."

He followed her inside the dark house as she dropped

her purse on the table. He stood close enough to catch her intoxicating scent, and had to fight to resist her as he followed her into the kitchen. Turning on only the under-counter lights, she busied herself filling the coffeemaker. Once finished, she turned around and looked up at him. "It'll take a few minutes to brew." She seemed nervous. "I had a good time tonight. The food was delicious."

Hell, she sounded about as unsure of this as he did. "I'm glad you enjoyed yourself."

She stepped closer. "I have you to thank for that. You made me feel…special."

"God, Gina. You have no idea how special you are." He couldn't stop himself—he pulled her into his arms and lowered his head. "Let me show you."

His lips brushed over hers and when he heard her gasp, he went back and captured her mouth. With her sweet body pressed against him, he lost any rational thoughts of going slow.

Gina followed his lead. Her arms circled his neck and she opened her mouth, allowing him to deepen the kiss. And he did. His tongue dove inside, brushing against hers, tasting and caressing. That only made him want more.

He finally tore his mouth away. "I've wanted to do that all night," he breathed, then continued the contact as he placed openmouthed kisses along her jaw, working his way to her graceful neck.

She sucked in a breath when he touched a sensitive spot. "Oh, Grady. I wanted you to kiss me, too."

"Let's see if we can keep agreeing."

He dipped his head and took her mouth again. She whimpered as he pulled her closer. The things this woman did to him made him forget everything.

Suddenly the sound of a phone startled them back to reality.

"I've got to get that." Gina pulled away and reached for the phone on the counter. "Hello?" She paused and said, "Lori, is something wrong with Zack?" She paused. "It's okay. I know you wouldn't call if it wasn't important."

Grady stepped away, trying to regain some control. Maybe letting things get this far wasn't a good idea. Gina wasn't ready.

He turned around when she ended the call. "I'm sorry, Grady. I've got to go get Zack. He's sick."

"I'll take you."

"You don't have to do that," she told him as they walked out the door. "Zack is my responsibility."

"If I drive you, then you can sit with him in the backseat."

She paused.

"Come on, Gina. You're wasting time." He guided her to his truck, realizing that the wind had picked up. There was rain in the air. "I'm a friend who wants to help you get your sick son home."

She finally smiled. "I hope you're not sorry that you volunteered."

Grady had a long list of things he was sorry about, but getting to spend more time with Gina Williams wasn't one of them.

Thirty minutes later Grady pulled up in front of Gina's house again. He got out and hurried around to the back door and opened it.

"Gina, go unlock the front door and I'll carry Zack inside."

She didn't argue and hurried up the walkway.

"Hey, Zack. Put your arms around my neck, and I'll carry you inside."

The boy groaned. "Grady, my stomach really hurts."

"It's going to be better, son. You'll be in your own bed."

No sooner had he lifted the boy out of the truck than Zack groaned, alerting Grady to what was about to happen. In a flash, Grady turned the child away as everything in his stomach came up and went all over the side of the truck and into the gutter.

"Well, that should make you feel better," he said.

Gina came running. "Grady, I'm sorry. Here, I'll take him."

"No, I got him." He took the handkerchief from his pocket, and gave it to the boy. "You finished?"

Zack managed a weak nod. "Yeah, I want to go to bed."

"You got it." Grady picked up his bundle and headed for the house. He carried him down the hall and into his bedroom. Placing him on the bunk bed, he stepped away and let Gina tend to her son.

Gina managed to help Zack into clean pajamas, get his mouth washed out and put him back into the bunk. She checked the window as she'd done every night since the kidnapping. It was starting to rain. A flash of lightning lit up the sky, reminding her that it was spring in Colorado.

"Are you going to be okay?" she asked her son.

He nodded. "I think I ate too much stuff at Aunt Lori's house."

She brushed back his hair. "Well, I'll be close by."

He snuggled under the blanket as the rain outside grew more intense, pounding against the roof. She kissed her son's head and realized he was already asleep.

She walked down the hall and into the kitchen, stopping suddenly when she saw Grady standing at the sink with his broad back to her as he washed up. In only his white T-shirt, she watched his toned muscles work across his broad shoulders and back as he washed up. Her gaze lowered to those killer black jeans that emphasized his narrow waist and hips.

She released a breath to calm her heart rate, glanced at his nice burgundy Western shirt wadded up on the table.

"I'm sorry. Is your shirt ruined?"

He turned around. "No, it just needs to be laundered."

She walked up to him. "Then I'll do it. That and apologize for Zack getting sick all over you."

"Believe me this hasn't been the first time. Through the years, I've held many a recruit's head over a latrine. Listening to them bellyache was a lot worse."

She couldn't get over this man. He took everything in his stride. "Well, as Zack's mother, I thank you for all your help."

The tension in the room was evident. Was he remembering earlier? Their kiss?

"I checked on Bandit, too," Grady told her. "He's fine, but I didn't know if he should stay in the utility room, or go to Zack's room."

"I've been trying to keep him on the porch."

"Good idea." He leaned back against the sink. "I should leave."

"But it's raining so hard."

His gaze remained on her. "If I don't, Gina—"

Suddenly lightning flashed and a loud crash of thunder sounded, then the lights flickered and went out.

"Oh, no." Instinctively, Gina started to go check on her child, but Grady stopped her.

"Bad idea to go running off without a flashlight." He felt his breath against her ear. "You have one?"

She couldn't think momentarily with him close, and touching her. "There's one in the drawer, the top one on the left."

He reached over her and his warmth seeped into her. It felt so good. Really good.

He pulled out the flashlight and turned it on. "I'll check on the boy. You stay put."

Once Grady left, Gina pulled herself together and found candles and matches. She lit them and had several arranged around the kitchen by the time Grady came back.

"Zack's sound asleep." He paused. "Looks like you're prepared."

For some things. She wasn't prepared for her feelings for him. "It's hard to tell how long the electricity will be out." She was chattering away aimlessly.

"Good idea," he told her as he made his way across the room.

Her pulse pounded in her ears, drowning out even the sound of the hard rain. She saw the smile he offered and it made her heart soar. So many emotions, she wanted to run, but she also wanted this man. "I know they might not be safe, but as long as we watch them, it should be okay."

"I'm afraid I'll be distracted," he said just as his head descended, then his lips touched hers. She sighed as the kiss deepened. She melted into him and let the sensations take over.

Grady felt an overwhelming desire as Gina moved against him. He couldn't stop feasting on her delicious mouth if his life depended on it. One kiss, two kisses weren't enough.

He tore his mouth away, then bent down and lifted Gina onto the counter. The soft glow of the candlelight only added to the intimacy.

He began raining kissing along her face to her ear. "You know where this is leading, don't you?"

She looked into his eyes and gave a nod.

"We need to *slow down*, Gina." He blew out a breath, not wanting to do anything to frighten her. "This is going too fast."

Gina wasn't sure if she knew what she was doing. She only knew that she wanted this man. "You make me feel things, Grady. Things I've never felt before."

Her hands moved up his chest over his T-shirt. She wanted so badly to touch his skin. She went to the hem of the shirt and slipped her hands underneath. The heat nearly burned through her as her fingertips made contact with his flat stomach.

For the first time she wasn't afraid of taking this next step…not with Grady. She tugged the shirt higher and leaned down to place a kiss against his skin. She felt the shiver along with his groan.

"Damn, Gina. If you are planning to drive me over the edge…"

Her own hands were trembling as she cupped his face. She leaned forward and placed a kiss against his lips. "I thought that was the point."

She went back for another kiss. She pulled the shirt higher and went for the center of his chest. Even in the candlelight, she could see the long puckered scar on his left side. It had to run from under his arm nearly to his waist.

"Oh, Grady," she cried on a whisper, feeling tears fill her eyes.

He quickly jerked down his shirt and stepped back. "Sorry, I should have warned you. It's pretty ugly."

"I'm not upset about what it looks like. Just the pain you must have endured."

He shook his head. She could see he was shutting down. "It was a long time ago." He released a breath and stepped back from her. She missed his warmth.

She got off the counter. "Grady…"

He didn't react to his name as he stood at the window. His broad shoulders were stiff, his back straight. She started toward him, but stopped, knowing the mood had changed. "Grady, I didn't mean to bring up bad memories."

"I don't have to look very far to be reminded of what happened that day."

She didn't know what to say to that, but she didn't have to—he made the choice for her.

"The rain has let up. I need to go."

She followed after him. "Grady, don't go."

He stopped at the door, but didn't turn around. "Gina, I'm not the man you need to teach you about anything. You'll need to find someone else for your next lesson."

CHAPTER ELEVEN

THE next day was Saturday and with Zack in tow, Gina went into the shop. While she'd felt lousy about how the date had turned out, something good had happened. Her son woke up this morning feeling great. He was also talking nonstop about Grady.

Since she hadn't slept much last night, she didn't feel much like conversing at all. She just wished she understood what had happened between her and Grady.

"Mom," Zack called to her. "Can I take Bandit for a walk?"

"Yes, but don't leave the block. Check back in twenty minutes." Old habits die hard. There was a time she wouldn't have let Zack out of her sight. Now, with Eric in jail, she knew they were safe. Plus she knew the town was filled with people who looked out for one another.

She closed the front door and turned her Open sign around and walked to the counter. Once again, her thoughts wandered back to Grady. After he had pulled back and walked out her door last night, she should have come to her senses. Besides, he wasn't going to be around much longer. How many times had he told her that? So maybe ending her crazy idea was for the best. Problem was, she wasn't interested in any man but Grady Fletcher.

The door of the shop opened and Lori walked in. "Hey, Gina," she called.

Her older sister was wearing a pair of black stretchy pants and a long pink polo shirt that showed off her blossoming pregnancy.

Gina went to greet her. "Lori. What brings you in?"

She hugged her. "I wanted to check on Zack. If he still wasn't feeling good, I'd take him off your hands. But since I ran into that happy kid outside, I see there's no reason. Cassie's helping him walk Bandit." She smiled. "Now we can talk." Her sister placed her hands on her hips. "So spill it. Is Grady Fletcher a good kisser?"

Gina felt her emotions churning inside. She shrugged as the bell over the shop door jingled and a woman walked in. Gina started to go to her, but Marie stopped her as she came in from the back and went to greet the customer.

"Come on." Lori took Gina by the arm and they headed toward the back for privacy. "You're not getting away with not telling me about your date."

Gina shrugged. "There's not much to tell. We had a nice dinner in Durango at Francisco's. He had steak and I had—"

"Stop," her sister said. "I don't need to know the menu. I saw how the man looked at you when you both came by the house to pick up Zack. So you can't tell me that he didn't kiss you once all night?"

"I didn't say that." Tears welled in her eyes. "I just don't think he wants to kiss me again. Ever."

Gina told her sister about what happened when they got back to the house.

"He might be insecure about the scar," Lori tried to assure her. "Does it bother you?"

Gina shook her head. "Of course not. We all have our scars." Gina couldn't stop the flood of awful memories of her marriage. Would she ever forget the things that Eric had done to her? Probably not, but she wanted to replace bad times with new, happy ones.

Lori drew her attention back. "Oh, honey, I wish I could have been there to help you more. To stop Eric."

"You were there for me, Lori."

Lori hugged her sister. "Well, I'm so proud of you. And thanks to your support group you're doing a lot better. If you ever need help getting to your meetings, just call me."

Gina smiled. "Thank you. You've always been there for me. It's time I do things for myself."

"Yes, it is. And I think Grady Fletcher is just the man who can be a positive force in your life."

"I think Grady has his own demons." She released a breath, knowing it was more than his physical scars. She'd seen the pain in his eyes.

Lori studied her. "You care about him a lot, don't you?"

She sighed. "I never planned to let it happen, but I can't seem to get him out of my head. He could break my heart, Lori."

"There's always that risk, sis. But if you don't go after what you want then you'll never know how wonderful it could be."

"Spoken like a happily married woman."

Lori grinned. "Yeah, I am. And I want you to find happiness, too. You and Zack deserve that."

Yes, they did. She thought about the mess she'd made of everything last night. "I'm not very good at this dating."

"While you're figuring it out, how about if I take

Zack home with me this afternoon while you work, then you can come by the house for supper?"

Gina had a funny feeling her sister was cooking up more than food. "You don't need to do that."

"I do, since I need a favor from you." She reached inside her oversize bag and pulled out a manila envelope. "These are papers for Joe Fletcher to sign. Would you give them to Grady so he can take them to him?"

Gina froze. *Go see Grady?* "Why don't you just take them to Shady Haven?"

"Because Joe asked me to give them to Grady first, so he can look them over."

"Why don't you have one of the bank employees do it?"

"I thought you were a bank employee."

"Come on, Lori. I've only staged a few bank-owned houses to sell."

Her sister shrugged. "Close enough." She walked to the door. "I'll go round up the kids and the dog. See you later." She paused at the door. "And take your time."

Great. Gina watched her sister leave. What was she going to do now? It would be a little too obvious when she showed up on Grady's doorstep.

Her assistant called to her. Marie walked over with a smile as the customer walked out the door. "You won't believe this. I just sold the Mersman pedestal table and the sideboard cabinet." She held up the credit card receipt so Gina could see the large amount charged. "Full price. She's even paying for us to deliver to Durango."

Gina glanced over the amount. "That's like two weeks' worth of sales."

"I know," Marie agreed.

Gina hated that Grady's things were disappearing

from the store. "Maybe you should call Grady and let him know."

Marie shook her head. "I think for half of this amount, you need to give the news to him in person."

"Where's that pretty Gina?" Joe Fletcher asked when Grady sat at the table at Shady Haven. The day was turning out to be nice so he'd wheeled his grandfather outside into the sunshine.

"I guess she's at her store, working."

The old man studied him and leaned down to give some attention to Scout. "You'd be wise to spend a lot of time with her before another man steals your claim."

Here we go again. "I have no claim on Gina."

"But you should, son. She's a keeper. I heard she's got a boy about eight."

Grady nodded. "His name is Zack. I found him in your mine, remember?"

"That's what I mean." Fletch raised an arthritic hand. "That young boy needs someone like you in his life."

Grady already knew the kid could use a father figure. "I'm not a family man."

"Says who? That ex-wife of yours? Look, Grady, I'm not an expert by any means, but—"

Grady interrupted. "But you're going to tell me anyway."

His grandfather glared at him. "Like I was sayin', I think you've had to take the blame for a lot of things that weren't your fault. Good Lord, son, you were off fighting a war, defending our freedom."

Grady had known before he'd left on his last deployment his marriage had been on shaky ground. So the pregnancy had been a shock, but he still had wanted to be there for his child. That was what he had trouble dealing with. "Look, Granddad, could we change the subject? Talking about it isn't going to change anything."

The old man studied him for a long time, then said, "Maybe it will. I've decided to stay here to live."

"At Shady Haven?" Grady asked.

His grandfather nodded. "They have apartments for seniors."

"Why? Isn't your hip healing correctly?"

"My hip is better than ever, and I've started therapy. It's not a walk in the park, but I'm handling it."

Grady was relieved.

"Once I'm on my feet, I'll be able to take care of myself. And here there are plenty of people my own age to keep me company."

Grady still wasn't buying this. "Are you sure this is what you want?"

Fletch nodded. "Yep, I'm too old to live up on that damn mountain."

"But you love it there."

A tired-looking Fletch turned to him. "I realized something, son. I was damn lonely."

That suddenly made Grady realize he'd neglected the one person who cared about him. "Granddad, I had no idea."

"No, son. I didn't even realize it myself until I came here and made some friends. We have a lot in common." He blew out a breath. "Besides, you'll be leaving soon, right?"

Now that his grandfather wouldn't be alone or lonely anymore, that would make his decision easier. Grady thought about Gina. How much he wanted her, but he knew in his heart, he wasn't the right man for her.

He nodded slowly. "What do you plan to do with the cabin and your properties?"

Fletch shrugged. "That's not my worry anymore. I've signed most everything over to you."

Gina wanted to turn around several times during her drive up the mountain. Once she saw Grady's truck, she knew there was no going back, especially when the man came walking out from behind the cabin. He was in his usual uniform, jeans and a black Henley T-shirt that made his shoulders look massive and his arms incredibly large. He had a towel draped over his shoulder, his hair was slicked back. He must have been in the shower. God help her, she thought as she got out of her car and walked up the path.

He looked concerned. "Gina, is there something wrong?"

"No." She put on a smile, seeing the droplets of water in his hair. "Sorry, didn't mean to disturb you."

He shrugged. "Since my shower is outside, I grab it during the warmest part of the day.

The picture of Grady with water sliding over his naked body flashed in her head. Her breathing grew labored.

"Gina, what brings you out here?"

She shook away the thought. "Marie sold the pedestal table and sideboard." She reached into her purse and realized her hands were a little shaky. She managed to take out the envelope with the check inside. "Here's your share of the sale."

Grady didn't take what she offered, but instead said, "Please, come in."

She walked up the steps and into the cabin, noticing right away how he'd kept the place clean and organized. She set her purse down on the kitchen table. She needed to make this quick and leave. "We got full price for both items."

He pulled the towel from his shoulder and took the check. "This is a nice profit."

"Yes, I appreciate you letting me sell them for you."

She locked on his deep-set brown gaze and it stole her breath. Why this man? She also noticed that he looked tired. Maybe he hadn't slept any better than she had. He caught her staring and frowned. She glanced away and pulled out the manila envelope from her large purse.

"Lori asked me to give you this," she said. "It's the legal papers on your grandfather's property." She hated feeling the tension between them. "She said you needed to have Joe sign them. But he wanted you to look them over."

"All right." He didn't open it. "The next time I visit."

"Okay. I should go." She nodded and turned toward the door, but never reached her destination.

Before she got there, Grady reached for her. "Gina."

She loved his hands on her, but had to resist. "Don't, Grady." She couldn't look at him. "Please, don't say anything. I'm sorry that I upset you last night. I never meant to." She ached inside as tears gathered in her eyes. Please, she couldn't cry in front of this man.

"You didn't upset me. I did that all by myself. You did everything right. That's the problem, Gina. I keep thinking that it would be so easy to let things happen between us." He turned her around to face him. "I want you, Gina Williams. That hasn't changed, but neither has the reality that I'm leaving here."

She felt brave. "Did I ask you to stay?"

Grady released her. "No, you didn't."

"I know your life is in Texas. Mine is here with my son." She wanted him to be a part of that family, too. "For the first time in a very long time, I'm making my own decisions on what I want to do." She took a step closer. "And I wanted you to show me what it's like to make love."

Grady was a little stunned by her declaration. "Gina, you're not thinking this through."

"Oh, but I have. You've been honest with me in saying you wanted me, and I'm saying that I want you to make love to me. To show me what it's like to feel tenderness, to be cherished by a man—"

Grady stopped her words when he reached for her and his mouth closed over hers. She could only manage a weak protest as he drew her into a tight embrace.

In no time at all, she became a willing participant, slipping her arms around his neck. His tongue ran along the seam of her lips and she parted them, allowing him to delve inside to taste her.

He finally tore his mouth away. His breathing labored. "God, Gina, this isn't a good idea. You deserve to be cherished and more." Grady searched her pretty face and her thoroughly kissed mouth, wishing he could give her the world.

"Damn, you're so sweet," he breathed, then went back for more because he couldn't seem to avoid the temptation. He pulled her against him, feeling all her curves, and backed up against the table. He lifted her and sat on the edge, then pulled her between his legs.

She whimpered and he immediately pulled away. "Did I do something wrong?"

Her pretty green eyes were glassy with desire. "No, it's just I've never felt like this before." She smiled shyly. "I like your hands on me. I like it when you touch me."

She took his large hand and brought it to the front of her sweater and placed it on her breast.

He cupped her weight in his palm and watched her eyes close, but not before he saw them darken with desire. "Oh, Grady."

He kissed her again, bringing her body against him. This was quickly getting out of hand.

"Gina, we're reaching the dangerous area here. My control is only so strong."

He found himself smiling at the fact that Josh wasn't going to be home until tomorrow. Cupping her face, he zeroed in on her big green eyes. "Gina, this is your decision. If you want this to go any further, it's your choice."

She leaned forward and placed a soft kiss on the scar on his neck. "I choose you, Grady Fletcher."

He shivered at her tender gesture, causing him only to want her more. "Then I suggest we move this off the table and into the bedroom."

He captured her mouth again in a hungry kiss, then scooped her up into his arms and carried her into the bedroom. The curtains were closed, leaving the room in shadows.

"I've been aching for you since that first night you slept out on the sofa."

He set her down next to the big brass bed.

"I didn't know," she said, sounding a little breathless.

He kissed her again. "It's a good thing."

Reaching for the hem of her sweater, he swept it off over her head, revealing her ivory lacy bra that barely hid the full breasts. His heart raced as he unfastened her jeans and slid them down to display the matching scrap of material that served as panties.

"Oh, darlin', you're lucky I didn't know what you had on underneath your clothes."

"You like?"

He gave her the once-over from her shapely legs up over her trim waist and flat stomach, then to her full breasts.

He wasn't going to survive this. "You have no idea."

She smiled shyly. "I was thinking about you when I bought them."

Grady took a steadying breath. He'd never felt desire like this before. He fought to keep it light. "Why, Miss Williams, are you trying to seduce me?"

"I have no idea what I'm doing." Her voice was husky. She reached for the three buttons at his neck and managed to open them. She looked up at him. "I don't want to do anything that bothers you, Grady." Her palms rested on his chest as her emerald gaze met his. "I have scars, too. Maybe not as visible as yours, but they're there just the same. Your scars were honorably earned, Grady. They could never change how I feel about you."

He remained silent as Gina took over and tugged the shirt from his jeans, then slipped her hands underneath. He sucked in a breath as her touch began to work magic. Then she took it further as she raised the shirt and placed her lips against his hot skin.

Once, twice… Oh, God. He was barely holding on to the last of his control when he jerked off the shirt, exposing the damages of war.

She looked at the puckered skin that ran from his shoulder to nearly his waist, then up at him. He saw the tears in her eyes. "Oh, Grady." She then leaned in and kissed the puckered skin. "How you suffered."

He didn't want to think about the past. Only now, with her. "You're making it feel a lot better." He lifted her onto the bed. "But right now that's not the area of my discomfort."

She smiled up at him. "Then maybe we should re-direct our efforts."

His mouth covered hers and he kissed her as he continued to show her how much he desired her. How much he would always desire her. That was the problem. Being with her like this was only going to make it harder to walk away.

CHAPTER TWELVE

THREE hours later Gina opened her eyes and discovered the sun was going down. She glanced at the clock beside the bed and saw that it was after six. And here she lay naked in bed, Grady Fletcher's arms wrapped around her waist, holding her close. She smiled, knowing she should be heading back to Destiny and dinner with Lori.

"Getting restless again?" Grady raised his head from the pillow, but didn't release her. "I thought the last time would keep you satisfied for a while."

She blushed, recalling they'd made love twice. Never had she been treated as if she were so special, so treasured. She rolled over and smiled at the sexy man.

"It was wonderful. But...I do have to pick up Zack. He's with Lori and Jace."

He frowned. "What if I won't let you go?" He pulled her close, letting her know he still desired her.

"I didn't say I wanted to leave." She cupped his face and pulled him down to meet her lips. And within seconds she let him know how much she meant those words.

He rose over her, bracing his arms on either side of her head. "That's some serious seduction tactics."

"So, Sarge, what are you going to do about it?"

Truthfully, Grady had no idea what he was going to

do with her, but at this moment, he wasn't going anywhere. "My best, ma'am."

He lowered his head and kissed her, once, twice, then his mouth began to move, trailing kisses, tasting her soft skin. He worked his way down over her breasts, lower to her flat stomach. That was when he caught the nearly invisible tiny white lines. Stretch marks. The proof she'd carried a baby in her womb. He closed his eyes and tried to push away the recurring memory about his own child. He paused and Gina's hands moved to his back.

"Grady?"

He raised his head. "Sorry." He rolled away, grabbed his jeans from the floor and slipped them on. "I guess you can call it a flashback."

He turned back to see she'd covered her body with the sheet. "It's okay, Grady."

He watched her eyes shift away from his gaze. "Oh, hell." He went back to her and sat on the bed. "It's not you, Gina. I know that sounds like a line, but it isn't. I carry around a lot of baggage."

She touched the side of his face. "Is there anything I can do to help you?"

"I just need some time." That was a lie. He hadn't been able to forget the pain or the guilt over the last few years. "I'm working through some things." He got up, grabbed his shirt off the floor and walked to the doorway. "I should go check on the dogs." Then he left.

Gina sat there stunned. What had happened? Okay, she wasn't so experienced that she could drive a man wild, but she thought together they'd been pretty incredible. She climbed out of the big bed and started pulling on her underwear. After she fastened her bra, she quickly dressed in her jeans and sweater. She should be getting home anyway. Her thoughts turned to Zack.

The safe way would be to forget about a relationship and focus on her life with her son. Grady Fletcher wasn't going to commit to her. She'd thought that was what she wanted until she realized how much she cared about him.

She passed the dresser and saw Grady's keys and coins tossed on the scarred surface. She also noticed the carved box and the corner of a photo hanging out. Okay, she was curious. She opened the lid and took hold of the grainy picture. A sonogram?

She looked closer and smiled seeing the familiar details of the baby. Who was this? She turned the photo over to the back and read, "Boy Fletcher" and the date. Several years ago.

She gasped. Grady had a child? She suddenly realized she wasn't alone in the room and glanced toward the doorway to find Grady.

"I'm sorry. I had no right." She put the picture back. "I should leave."

Grady came inside the room and took the picture. He wasn't sure why he was so angry. "Come on, Gina. Don't stop now. Don't you want to know who this is?"

She swallowed. "Only if you want to tell me."

His chest tightened, but he got the words out. "That's my son."

"You have a child?"

"*Had.* That's the operative word, Gina. Had."

"What happened to him?"

Here came the hard part. "My wife went into early labor…he was stillborn."

She gasped. "I'm so sorry."

"So am I. I was told that no one was to blame for what happened."

Grady remembered the two days it had taken him to get across the globe, to be there for Barb, for his son.

He couldn't look at Gina. "That's what the doctor told me once I got there two days later. I was overseas when my wife was delivering our baby."

He closed his eyes, and could see the long hospital corridors as his footsteps echoed when he ran from the elevator to the nursery, but there wasn't a Fletcher baby behind the glass. Finally the nurse sent him to see his wife in her room. He found her, all right. She was packing her clothes and about to go home with her parents. When he went to her, she pushed him away.

"You're too late, Grady," she cried. "Too late for your son. And too late for us." She'd walked out the door.

He opened his eyes and met Gina's gaze. "Don't make that mistake, Gina. Don't depend on me. I'll let you down."

"How could you know your wife was going into labor early?"

He shook his head.

"Did she keep the pregnancy from you?" she asked.

"No, but it wasn't planned, either." He sighed. "When things started to turn bad in the marriage, I chose another deployment, instead of staying and trying to work through our problems."

"The army was your job. Surely your wife knew that when she married you."

Gina went to Grady, wondering who'd been there for him to help him grieve over his child. She reached for him and felt him tense, but she ignored his resistance. She wrapped her arms around his waist and laid her head against his chest. She shed tears for the father and the child.

"I'm sorry that you never got to hold your son. That

you never got to say goodbye." His grip tightened around her and she felt his tears drop against her cheek. She never dreamed she could love a man as much as she loved Grady Fletcher. She held on to him a few minutes until he finally loosened his grip and moved away.

Once he composed himself, he turned back to her. "Thank you."

"Any time."

He started to say more when his cell phone rang. He pulled it out. "Hey, Josh." He answered it as he walked away.

Gina put the treasured picture back in its special place, then pulled the bed together before she walked back into the main room.

"Okay, I'll see you back here tomorrow," Grady said into his phone. "Goodbye." He hung up.

Embarrassed that she hadn't given a thought to Grady's housemate, she blurted, "Oh, I forgot all about Josh."

"I didn't. He went to Texas to check out places for our kennel."

Suddenly reality hit her. Grady was still leaving.

He noticed her surprise, too. "I told you from the beginning, I was opening our business in Texas."

"I know, but a girl can always hope."

He came to her. "Gina. I can't tell you how special you've become to me, but… I've tried to make a go of settling down before."

She hurt a lot. "Can't say you didn't warn me." She forced a smile. "Hey, it was fun." She worked hard to hide her blush. "And this afternoon…was incredible." She glanced around for her purse and grabbed it to make her escape. "I've got to go. Maybe before you leave town you'll stop by and say goodbye."

He took her arm and stopped her. "Gina. Don't do this. You mean too much to me—"

She stopped his words of regret. "Just not enough to stay around."

"I told you before—"

"Believe me, I heard everything you said." She released a breath. "Too bad for you, Master Sergeant Fletcher, because there's a guy out there who's going to want to stick around for me."

"And that's what you deserve."

"It's something we all deserve, Grady, but first, you have to forgive yourself, realize you deserve happiness, too."

She swung around and walked out praying she could make it to her car. Once down the road, she pulled off and burst into tears. She'd lost everything she'd ever wanted in a man.

By the next morning Grady's bad mood hadn't improved at all. Even the dogs wanted no part of him. Add in no sleep and too much coffee, there was no hope that things would change anytime soon.

"Break time, boys," he called to the dogs. "Get your toys."

The shepherds took off and Scout was the first back with the yellow tennis ball. The animal dropped it on the ground and Grady threw it to the far end of the pen while he kept telling himself he'd done the right thing by letting Gina go yesterday.

He felt his chest constrict as he continued to toss the ball. She had no idea how hard it had been to lie to her, to tell her he didn't want her or her kid.

Hell, he was already involved whether he liked it

or not, but she'd already had one jerk in her life—she didn't need another.

He closed his eyes and could still picture her in that big bed. Her sweetness nearly drove him over the edge. Yet, everything she did pleased him. He'd never... He shook away the wondering thought.

Damn, he had to get out of here and back to Texas.

He called to Scout, Beau and Rowdy. "Time to get to work," he told them.

He'd only been at it for about ten minutes when he saw an SUV pull up and Justin Hilliard got out.

The businessman was dressed in dark pleated trousers, a white shirt and striped tie. He walked through the rough terrain as if he had on boots instead of expensive Italian loafers.

Grady shook his hand. "Hey, Hilliard. What brings you out to my neighborhood? Come to see how the other half lives?"

The sarcasm didn't seem to bother the visitor. "I came by to see you, Grady," he said as he stopped beside the waist-high gate. "I just finished a meeting down in Durango with my new mountain bike instructor, Brian Connelly. He's retired now from the pro circuit, so running my school is perfect for him." The man grinned. "Also he'll be designing mountain bikes which I'll be manufacturing right here in Destiny."

Grady felt extreme envy for the man who just about had everything, not his money as much as his pretty wife and children. "Seems all your dreams are coming true."

"Yeah, I've been a lucky guy. That's why I can afford to spread my good fortune around."

That piqued his interest and Hilliard saw it. "You haven't stopped by to see me, Grady."

"I've been busy. Mostly I'm not interested."

"I'm not going to let you off the hook, not until you hear me out."

Did this man ever give up? "I've already heard your spiel."

"A lot has changed since we last talked. Seems your grandfather owns some of the property I want."

Grady sent the dogs off to play as he walked out the gate to the pen. "You want this property?"

Hilliard shook his head. "The three acres just north of town. I'd planned to buy that section when Billy Hutchinson's name was on the deed, but Lorelei Yeager discovered that Joe Fletcher is the true owner. Now it seems he's transferred the title to you."

This was getting interesting. "Is that so?"

Justin nodded. "I already own the adjoining land, but I'd like to extend my trails. I want to buy your property. Question is, what's it going to cost me?"

"I haven't even had a chance to look over the land in question."

"It's definitely a prime area. I don't want to develop it, if you're worried," Justin insisted. "I want to keep the land in its natural state, except for bike trails. Do you think we could work out some kind of deal?"

A dozen things rushed though Grady's head. The sale would cut the ties here in Destiny. He could take the money for his project in Texas.

"I have another idea, Grady," Justin told him. "Since the land is a heavily wooded area, it could work for other things, too. Like training rescue dogs." He glanced around the temporary structures Grady had built. "You could build a real kennel there, too."

"That could take a lot of money."

"It's going to take money in Texas, too. It's hotter

there and doesn't have these mountain views, or my offer of leasing your dogs for the winter months."

Or Gina. Grady hated that the man had him thinking of changing his plans.

Hilliard checked his watch. "Look, I've got to go now—my son has baseball tryouts." He smiled. "I can't miss it."

Another dose of envy hit Grady. "Then you should go."

"I still want to talk to you about this some more. Could you meet up later with me and Jace Yeager? Say about eight o'clock at the Rocky Top Saloon in town? We can talk over a few beers. I'm buying."

"Look, I can't promise you anything. I have a partner."

"I know." Justin began backing away. "Bring Josh along, and we'll all talk."

"Good luck to your son," Grady called.

"Thanks, I appreciate it."

Grady watched the man leave and he thought about Zack. How would he do today? He found himself putting the dogs into the kennels and heading down to town. What would it hurt just to check on the boy?

Gina walked around her empty house that evening, restless. Zack was spending the night with Ryan Hilliard. They'd been picked to be on the same baseball team today, so they were best friends now. She smiled, feeling so blessed that Tim Keenan had volunteered to be the team's coach.

She might be Zack's mother, but she had no idea how to encourage her nearly eight-year-old's new love for the game. She'd tried to help, but Zack hadn't wanted her to go, and Uncle Jace was working. She thought about

Grady, but she couldn't impose on him any longer, not after yesterday. All her worries had been unfounded, though, when Zack came home beaming with news of his day. Her son's life seemed to be perfect now.

Hers was a mess. She recalled how Grady had made it clear that he didn't want her in his life. She could survive the rejection, but if he stayed in town... She blinked away threatening tears. She didn't want him to leave at all. She loved the man, and she probably would for a long, long time.

There was a knock on the door and she looked out the peephole to see her sister. She quickly let her inside.

"Lori, what are you doing here?"

"We both have the night off from kids. Zack's at a sleepover, Jace has a business meeting, and Cassie is staying with Maggie."

Gina smiled, remembering the housekeeper from Hutchinson House who'd helped raise Lori when she was a child. "How is Maggie adjusting to her new apartment?"

"She's doing fine, but I had to insist that she hire more help when the mansion is rented out for functions." Lori waved her off. "Hey, I just got a call from Paige to meet her and Morgan at the Rocky Top Saloon. You wanna come with us?"

Gina wasn't in the mood to go anywhere. "I think I'll pass."

"Why?" Her sister placed her hands on her hips. "You aren't moping around over a man, are you?"

Gina started to deny that Grady was the reason for her misery. Her sister wouldn't buy it anyway.

"Okay, give me five minutes to change."

At eight o'clock Grady and Josh walked into the Rocky Top Saloon. There was a large entry with a bar on one side and the dining room on the other. The entire place had the look of a hunting lodge with hardwood floors and open beamed ceilings, not to mention the elk and deer heads mounted on the knotty-pine-paneled walls. Country music poured out of the jukebox, but he managed to hear his name called out.

Justin stood across the room past the small dance floor toward the back. He nudged Josh and they walked over.

"Hey, glad you two could make it," Justin said.

Grady nodded as he introduced Josh.

Hilliard did more introductions. "Grady and Josh, you remember Jace, and of course, Reed. And this is Brian Connelly."

Grady shook hands all around. "Good to meet you," he said to the new guy.

Hilliard ordered another pitcher of beer as Grady sat. It was Connelly who began the conversation.

"I hear you're retired army."

Grady nodded. "Got out in December."

Josh added his similar résumé.

"Well, all I can say is thank you both for your service."

Grady nodded and took a sip of the beer that had been placed in front of him while Hilliard filled Josh in on his ideas for a kennel in Destiny.

Brian cornered Grady. "Justin told me about your dogs."

For the next twenty minutes every guy at the table was talking up all the good qualities of the town. Grady couldn't deny that Hilliard had a well-crafted plan for his biking school, riding trail and snow adventures. He put down some numbers for the property that were also impressive.

Grady leaned back in his chair. Okay, he couldn't help but think about it. Damn, it looked profitable on paper, and then he was surprised when Hilliard offered to be a silent partner in the rescue dog business.

Grady exchanged a glance with Josh. He looked curious, and Grady was once again thinking about the deal. There was only one person keeping him from signing. Gina. Could he live in this town and be around her all the time?

"Hey, Reed?" Jace called. "Did you tell our wives where we were meeting?"

Grady and all the men turned toward the door. That's where they saw four of the prettiest women in town. Morgan Hilliard, Paige Larkin, Lori Yeager and Gina.

CHAPTER THIRTEEN

GINA felt a warmth pulse through her as Grady's hand pressed against her waist as he escorted her to the dance floor. Silently he took her into his arms and began to move to the music. She couldn't resist and leaned into him, inhaling his scent, a mixture of soap and what she knew to be pure Grady.

She also liked the familiar feel of his body molded against hers. The heat of his skin, and the strength of his hands, hands that had touched every inch of her flesh just days ago…

She shivered.

"Are you okay?" he asked against her ear.

No! "Yes, I'm fine."

She closed her eyes, recalling the look on his face when she'd walked up to the table. He didn't want to see her here tonight. That hurt. She knew he was only her dance partner out of obligation. He hadn't been given a choice when all the other couples had got up.

"You don't have to do this, Grady." Okay, so she wanted to be in his arms, just not this way.

He pulled back. "Since I left the army, I've been pretty much making my own decisions."

She nodded, then glanced away.

He touched her chin, making her look at him. "Believe me, Gina, holding you in my arms has never been a hardship."

To prove the point, he pulled her close as George Strait sang about getting to "Amarillo by Morning." She didn't want to listen to the lyrics. Grady was leaving soon. That she had to accept, but it didn't stop the hurt.

She felt his arm tighten around her waist as he pulled her closer against him, his strength making her remember how gentle his touch could be, how loving.

The song changed to Lady Antebellum singing "Need You Now." Grady's hold tightened as their feet shuffled back and forth in the crowd of dancers. Then she felt his mouth against her ear. His warm breath caused her to shiver. Why was he doing this? Why couldn't he leave her alone?

Gina pulled back. "I can't… I've got to go." She moved through the couples dancing on the floor. Once at the table, she grabbed her purse and headed for the door.

Grady cursed, then made his way through the crowd, finally catching up with Gina at the door. With several couples nearly blocking the area, he escorted her outside and to a private spot.

"Gina, I'm sorry. I didn't know you'd be here."

She finally looked up at him. "I know. I'm sorry I spoiled your fun."

He ran fingers through his hair. "Dammit, Gina. It wasn't supposed to be fun. Justin said it was a relaxed business meeting, and then we looked up to see their wives." He met her gaze. "And you…"

"Well, I'm going home so you can go back and finish the meeting. Enjoy the evening." She took off down the street.

Grady hurried after her. "Gina, let me drive you."

She shook her head. "No, I'm not your responsibility. Besides, I can handle the short walk."

Damn stubborn woman. "I have no doubt you can, but at least let your sister know that you're going home."

He was rewarded with a furious look. "I'm not going back inside." She took out her phone and punched in the number. "Lori, I'm going home." There was a pause. "No, you stay. Grady's taking me." She ended the call and dropped it back into her purse. "Okay, you're relieved of duty," she told him and marched off.

What the hell? He went after her. "What do you think you're doing?"

"I'm walking up Main Street, then making a right on Maple, then a left on Cherry Street."

He ignored her smart answer. "So you lied to your sister."

"I don't want her to worry." They stepped off the curb and started down the next block, passing the town square and the sheriff's office. The parking lot was well lit, so was the street.

"What if something happened to you?"

She stopped and faced him. "Look, Grady, you have to quit doing this. Stop playing hero. Stop thinking you have to rescue me. I'm trying really hard to take control of my life. Do things on my own, to be independent."

He arched an eyebrow. "And I'm interfering with that?"

"Yes. You are."

"What if I just want to do the gentlemanly thing and walk a lady home?"

She threw up her arms in exasperation. "I give up."

Well, he wasn't going to and he followed her as she walked on.

Ten minutes later they ended up on her porch. "Okay,

I'm home safe and sound." She slipped her key into the lock. "Good night, Grady."

"Gina," he whispered her name, hoping to get her to turn around and look at him. No such luck.

Still she faced the door. "What, Grady?"

"I'm headed for Texas in a few days."

In the soft glow of the porch light, he saw her tense. "Have a safe trip."

"Gina, it's for the best."

She swung around. "You call running away the best solution? Well then, go for it. But I think what you're doing is giving up. A second chance at a home, a family with a grandfather who loves you. But go. I hope whatever you're looking for makes you happy."

She stared at him for what seemed to be an eternity, and he couldn't stand it anymore.

He pulled her into his arms and held her. She felt so good, too good. He kissed the side of her face and quickly worked to her tempting lips.

"Grady…"

He ignored her as he covered her mouth in a heated kiss. He just needed one more taste of what he had to give up. She gave the soft moan he knew so well, but he resisted taking any more. He tore his mouth away. "Goodbye, Gina."

"Goodbye, Grady." She turned and walked inside. He just stood there, aching to go after her. Instead he started down the steps when he heard something. Moving back to the door, he recognized the sound of her crying. His chest tightened. Oh, God, he'd never wanted to hurt her. He started to knock, but paused, knowing he had too many things he had to deal with first. Instead he turned and walked away. Again.

* * *

It was a beautiful spot.

The next day Grady walked along the edge of his grandfather's property and glanced up at the picturesque San Juan Mountains. The sky was so blue it took your breath away. He also liked that so much of the area was densely wooded. He glanced at Josh and he seemed just as intrigued with it, too.

Justin caught up to them. "I can't believe you want to leave all this." The businessman shook his head. "Seems you two could have it all." He pointed off toward the woods. "What a training ground. And you can put your kennels at the base, right off the highway. You're far enough away your dogs wouldn't bother my training facility, or the guests. And we wouldn't bother your dogs."

Grady was thinking about it. "It's beautiful."

"I agree. You've got a sweet parcel of land, Grady," Hilliard told him. "Look at the spot over there." He pointed to the crest of the hill. "You could build a house there and have views all around."

With the idea of a home came thoughts of Gina. How would she like it here?

No, he had to push any thoughts of her aside, not think about what he couldn't have.

He turned to Josh. "What about you?"

"I think this is a great place," Josh said, and looked at Grady. "And it seems to me that owning the land already eliminates a big expense, and frees up more money for dogs. Maybe hire an employee to help with the upkeep. We can concentrate on the training. Whatever you decide, Sarge, I'll go along with it."

That was the lead-in Justin needed. "Look, if you're reluctant about selling any of your land to me for my training facility, how about we lease the section from you?" His hand made a sweeping motion. "And you don't lose any of this."

So tempting, Grady thought. "I need to think about it. Can you give me a few days?"

Justin nodded and walked away with Josh, leaving Grady alone with his thoughts, his dreams and what he couldn't have that kept it all from being perfect.

Little League practice was the next afternoon, and Grady found he couldn't stay away. Despite him leaving for Texas in the morning, he wanted to see how Zack was doing.

He parked on the far side of the baseball field and got out to watch the last of the practice. Tim Keenan and Jace Yeager were the coaches, but when he saw Gina's brother-in-law, he thought he'd better leave.

He headed back to the truck when he heard someone call him. He turned to see Zack running toward him.

"Grady, aren't you going to help me today?"

"Well, it looks like you have enough help already."

Tim came up to him. "We can always use another hand."

Grady looked at Jace. After a few seconds he motioned for him to join them. "Okay, what do you want me to help with?"

Tim smiled. "Jace has fielding, and I'm working with them on running the bases. So how about hitting?"

Thirty minutes later, Grady finally thought Zack was making some progress. He was a quick study.

"That's it son, keep your eye on the ball." He pitched a ball to Zack. The first one he missed, but he made contact with the second and the third. "That was great." They exchanged high fives.

The kid beamed. "You showed me real good, Grady."

He felt the pride for the boy's achievements. Finally, Tim called a halt to the practice and they finished with drinking bottles of cold water. Soon the kids went off with their parents. Zack turned to him. "I'm having my birthday party next Saturday. Will you come, Grady?"

"Oh, Zack. I'm not sure I'll be here. I have to leave town for a few days."

The boy's face dropped. "Oh, I wanted to show you some tricks I taught Bandit."

Grady knew he didn't want to encourage the boy, then have to disappoint him. "I bet they're good tricks, too. Maybe I'll stop by the house when I get back."

"So you are coming back."

With his nod, the boy said, "Okay."

Hearing Zack's name called, Grady turned to see Gina. She was walking across the field, but when she spotted him, she stopped. His gaze surveyed the petite woman in jeans and a sweater. Just like every time other time he looked at her she affected him like no other woman. How long would it take to stop wanting her? Never.

Gina raised a hand and waved to her son. "Come on, Zack," she called. "We need to get home."

"I got to go." Zack went to him and threw his arms around his waist. "Thanks for helping me today. Bye, Grady."

The boy ran off to his mother. When he reached her, Gina put her arm around her son and they walked off together. Grady had to resist running after them both. The pain in his chest spread to his heart as the two most important people walked out of his life.

"Those two are really special."

He glanced at Tim Keenan. "Yeah, they are. I need to go."

"I'll walk with you to the parking lot," Tim said. "I couldn't help but overhear you tell the boy you're leaving town."

Grady nodded. "I'm going to look at some property in San Antonio." Although he knew staying here would be better all around, he needed to make a clean break from Gina. "It's close to the base where we can get more dogs."

Tim nodded. "I guess a convenient location is important." There was a pause. "I would think staying here would be even more convenient, especially with your grandfather here and other special…friends."

Grady stopped. "Look, Tim, I know you're trying to help, but this is best for everyone."

Tim nodded toward Gina's car as it drove out of the lot. "I know there are at least two people who don't feel that way."

Later that evening Grady sat in his grandfather's room at Shady Haven.

"So you're really gonna go?" Fletch asked, not looking happy.

This wasn't getting any easier. "You knew I was leaving eventually."

"Hell, son, an old man can hope."

Grady noticed the sadness in his eyes. "I'm sorry, Granddad."

"I can deal with you leaving again, Grady, if it's for the right reasons. And if it makes you happy."

"It's for my business." God, he was a lousy liar.

"Let's at least be honest, son. My eyesight isn't so bad that I can't see you care about that pretty Gina Williams."

Damn, he didn't want to do this. "Look, Fletch, I

know you want me to stay here, but…" Grady wasn't sure if he could be around Gina and Zack. "I'm not sure I fit in to all this family stuff."

Fletch looked sad as he shook his head. "I blame your parents for that. After their divorce, I wanted you to live with me permanently, not just those summers when your dad didn't have time for you."

Grady swallowed back the emotions clogging his throat. "I know."

"You always tried so hard to keep your distance, son. You wouldn't let anyone get close." He paused. "Not all people are out to hurt you like your parents, or your ex-wife."

Grady tensed. He didn't want to rehash any of this. "I tried to play the family man before—it didn't work."

His grandfather watched him, then said, "I wish I was wise enough to give you all the right answers, son, but I can't. I lost your grandmother too soon. I didn't want to try to find someone again." Those kind hazel eyes stared at him. "That was a mistake. I was a lonely man for a lot of years."

"At least your marriage wasn't a failure. I've done so many things wrong."

"People make mistakes, son."

The pain was nearly overwhelming. "I was never home…not even when my son was born." He felt his throat closing up. "He didn't survive."

Fletch leaned forward and gripped his grandson's hand. "Oh, Grady, I'm so sorry." The old man was silent for a long time then said, "As tragic as it was to lose a child, you can't blame yourself for what you have no control over."

Grady didn't want to hear excuses. "I should have been there."

"Of course you should have been there for your wife. But, son, would it have changed the outcome?" Fletch asked.

He shook his head, unable to say the words.

"We can't live on what-ifs, son." His grip tightened. "You'll always grieve for your child, but it's time to forgive yourself, too. Let people help you," Fletch told him. "Maybe that special someone."

"Gina."

Fletcher shrugged. "I just thought that she would be someone you could build a future with. And what's not to like about a seven-year-old kid? Seems to me, that boy could use a good male role model in his life."

His heart ached. He couldn't stop himself from wanting the same thing. "I failed before."

"You weren't alone in your first marriage, so don't take all the blame." There was a long pause, then his grandfather said, "Gina's marriage was a tragic one, but she trusts you. That's because she sees what I see, a good man. Love with the right person can heal a lot of wounds," the old man added.

Grady felt a glimmer of hope. He'd never planned on another relationship, and then along came Gina and he couldn't get her out of his head, out of his heart. And she made him want to reach for that dream.

Grady thought back to the afternoon Gina had held him and cried with him for his child. How her touch had comforted him, how it had soothed his scarred body. How she had made him feel...loved. He closed his eyes and took a shaky breath. God, he loved her, and all he did was reject her. Would she ever forgive him for that? Take a chance on him?

He had to convince her. He suddenly realized how

badly he wanted to make a life with her and Zack. How badly he wanted to stay right here in Destiny.

He stood and smiled at Fletch. "Do you think you could put up with me hanging around?"

The old man grinned. "Maybe if you bring Gina around to see me once in a while, and I wouldn't mind getting a great-grandkid or two out of it." He arched an eyebrow. "You need me to put in a good word for you?"

"No, I think I can handle that part," he said, though deep down he wasn't so sure. He had to repair a lot of damage.

Two days later Gina had been at work for an hour at the thrift shop. Since 7:00 a.m. She'd managed to get a lot done, too, including moving another reupholstered sofa to the display window.

"Marie, your work is incredible," Gina told her as they stood back and enjoyed the view.

"What are you talking about? You redesigned it. The sofa looks totally different."

"Well, you did most of the sewing. So why don't you take the rest of the day off?"

"Oh, no. I'm fine, really. I have a ton of work to do here."

"Not today. Take the baby to the park. You need some sunshine. Go."

The woman didn't argue, and within ten minutes Gina was alone. Oh, boy. Maybe that wasn't such a good idea. She had too much time to think.

"Do some paperwork." She went behind the counter and picked up the receipts from yesterday and started to head back to the office when the bell signaled over the front door. She glanced up to see Grady Fletcher.

Her breath caught as the tall man dressed in jeans and a collared shirt walked in.

Oh, God. What was he doing here?

He looked as nervous as she felt. "Hello, Gina."

"Grady."

He shut the door and flipped the Open sign to Closed. Then he locked it before he walked over to her.

"What are you doing?"

"I'd like to talk to you. So I need a few minutes of uninterrupted time."

"And I have a business to run." She started to walk past him when he reached for her.

"Please, Gina. It's important."

Those dark eyes bored into hers. "Funny, you didn't have time for me when you needed to leave town."

"I didn't leave," he said.

She froze. "Why not?"

"I had things to do here. To settle."

She felt the imprint of his hand on her arm. She pulled away. "So when do you leave?"

"I'm not going to Texas."

Those words got her attention.

He glanced around. "Could Marie watch the shop for an hour or so? I want to show you something."

"Marie isn't here."

Then she heard the voice from the back room. "I'm here, Gina." She walked in from the back, pushing the stroller. "I returned to get my purse." She looked at Grady. "If it's for a good cause, I don't have a problem staying a few hours."

"A very good cause."

Grady turned back to Gina. She looked so pretty it took his breath away. Stay focused. He glanced over her jeans and pink blouse and tennis shoes.

"Good, you're dressed for where I have to take you."

She still resisted. "Who said I'm going anywhere?"

He stopped. "I'll make it worth your while. You can have all the furniture in the cabin." When she still didn't move, he added, "Please, Gina. If it wasn't important, I wouldn't ask you."

"You have no idea what you're asking of me."

"I do. I'm hoping you still trust me enough to give me this chance."

She sighed. "Okay, I'll go." She glanced at Marie. "But I won't be gone long."

To Grady she said, "This had better be important."

He nodded, staring into those mesmerizing green eyes. "It's the most important thing I've ever done."

CHAPTER FOURTEEN

TEN minutes later they were going out of town, and at first Gina wondered if they were headed to the cabin.

No! She couldn't go back there. There were too many memories. Before she could protest, Grady drove by the turnoff. Instead they passed the new construction site that was Jace's new project.

"Isn't that the new mountain bike training center?"

"Yes. They're moving fast to complete it by mid June. Justin already has twenty students enrolled."

Gina studied the man behind the wheel. With the cowboy hat pulled low, she had trouble reading him. Why did he want her to come along? Better question, why had she consented to go with him?

He pulled off the road and into a clearing, then parked. "We're here," he announced as he climbed out and hurried around to her side. She had no choice but to take his offered hand to help her out of the truck.

"Come on." He didn't release his hold as he walked her to the edge of the hill.

She didn't want to think about the warmth of his large hand engulfing hers. How safe and utterly feminine he made her feel.

She concentrated on the beauty before her. Miles of

pine and cedar trees covered the mountain range—the peaks looked as if they could touch the rich blue sky.

"It's breathtaking." That wasn't a lie, but why was she here?

He turned to her. "You really like it?"

"What's not to like?"

"This is where I'm building Sarge's Rescue Dogs and Kennel." He pointed off in the distance. "Well, it's actually going to be over there."

Her heart raced as she fought to contain her excitement. "So you decided against Texas."

"I weighed the options." His dark gaze locked on hers and held for a long time. "This is my grandfather's land. He gave it to me. Then Justin offered me a good deal to help my business—even Josh encouraged me. It seemed impractical to leave."

Well, that was just great. "Good for you. It's a lovely spot." How would she deal with Grady staying, running into him around town?

"I'm happy for you, Grady. Now, could you please take me back?" She started to leave when he stopped her.

"Not so fast. I haven't finished telling you everything."

He'd said enough. She didn't want to hear about his new life here. How he'd moved on and didn't need her in his life. "Grady. Please." She turned and marched back to the truck.

"Gina, wait," he called.

She ignored him as she reached for the passenger door, when he caught up and stopped her from opening it. He stood so close that Gina couldn't move. His breath was warm against her neck.

"You aren't even going to hear what else I have to say?"

She didn't turn around to look at him, just shook her head.

"You don't want to hear that I plan to build a place on the crest over there. How I want the whole back side of the house to be glass so you can see that view from every room."

"Sounds lovely. Can I leave now?"

"Not before I tell you—"

"Stop." Gina swung around. "I'm glad you've moved on, Grady. Okay." She hated that tears filled her eyes. "I just don't need to hear—"

Her words were smothered when his mouth closed over hers. She moaned and gripped the front of his shirt, and in her weakened state, allowed Grady to have his way. She'd missed him so much. The feelings he created in her.

He broke off the kiss. "I've missed you, Gina. God knows, I tried to stay away, tried to let you find someone who would be better for you than a set-in-his-ways ex-army guy. But I discovered that I want you, only you."

Even though his confession thrilled her, it wasn't enough. "Grady. I can't deny I want you, too." She couldn't help but think about their little time together. "But I want more than some stolen hours."

He pulled back and his hard gaze locked on hers, then he stepped back.

"I want more, too, Gina." He still looked uneasy. "I know it's hard for you because of your bad marriage. And my track record in that department was lousy."

She frowned when he backed away. She watched as he pulled off his hat, raking fingers through his hair.

"Grady," she called to him. "Tell me why you brought me here."

He turned back to her. "I'm not good at this, Gina. In the army, you're given orders and you carry them out."

"Then consider this an order and tell me what you have to say."

Grady felt his palms sweat, his heart race. Hell, he felt like a teenager.

"I want to stay in Destiny, be close to my grandfather. Build my business here." His gaze met hers. "But most importantly, Gina, I want to build a life with you."

"But I thought you wanted to leave so badly," she finally said. "That you weren't the man for me. You couldn't give me what I needed."

He blew out a breath. So she wasn't going to make this easy. He thought about Tim Keenan's advice. He straightened and walked toward her. "That was before I realized that I could give you more than any man." His throat suddenly went dry. "Because no one could love you as much as I do."

Gina blinked, then he saw the tears in her eyes. "Oh, Grady."

He stepped closer. "Is that a good 'Oh, Grady' or a bad 'Oh, Grady'?"

She smiled. "It's good." She rushed into his arms. "I love you, too, Grady Fletcher."

He tossed his cowboy hat into the back of the truck, then reached for her. "Those are the sweetest words I ever heard," he whispered right before his mouth captured hers.

There was no way he could ever express the depth of his feelings for her, but he was going to try. He pulled her tighter against him, letting her know how much he desired her, wanted to cherish her for a lifetime.

He pulled back, but didn't let her go. He cupped her face tenderly. "I meant what I said, Gina. I want a future with you and Zack. I know you've gone through a lot. You can have all the space you need to heal, just know I'll be there. I want you to trust me that I'll never hurt you intentionally."

She kissed him sweetly. "I know that, Grady. I've known that from the first." She reached up and touched the scar on the side of his neck. "That afternoon when we made love, everything you shared with me, I know it was painful for you, both physically and emotionally." Her gaze met his, but he felt the connection deep down into his soul. "I've never felt that way…ever. Being with you was so special."

"I want to make you feel that way always," he said. "I want to marry you, Gina." He saw her surprised look. "Okay, maybe it's too early for that step. But I want to be your husband, your partner and Zack's father."

This time the tears did fall. "Oh, Grady."

He searched her face. "Again, is that good or bad?"

She nodded. "Oh, definitely good." She cupped his face. "You'll be a wonderful father… One any child would be proud of." She knew he was thinking about the son he'd lost. "Zack is going to be so lucky to have you."

"No, I'm the one who's lucky to have you both." He took a steady breath, then knelt on the ground in front of her. "Gina Williams, I love you more than I ever thought possible. Would you do me the honor to marry this old soldier? I promise to love and cherish you forever."

Her eyes widened at his proposal. "Oh, yes, Grady, I'll marry you." She leaned down and placed her mouth against his. With a groan, he stood, wrapping her in his arms and kissed her until they were both breathless.

"Oh, Grady, I'm so happy."

"Enough to play hooky with me for the rest of the day?"

Gina looked up at the handsome man who was going to be her husband. "Sounds tempting." She hesitated. "I guess I could call Marie and have her close the shop. So what do you have in mind?"

"I could lie and say we have a lot to discuss, but I have a feeling we'll get distracted the second we're alone." He grinned at her and she couldn't resist.

"So you're saying you can make it worth my while?"

"I'm a soldier, I don't back down from a challenge. Especially someone as tempting as you."

She gave him a soft kiss and turned in his arms. Together they looked at the view as she pointed toward the ridge. "You said you're building a house there?"

"Our house," he corrected. "First, though, I need to finish the kennel for the dogs, which Jace said would be complete by summer's end." Grady smiled. "Then we can break ground on our home. We want to get as much done as we can before winter." He leaned down and kissed the side of her neck. "I want to do everything quickly so it's ready for you and Zack."

"How soon do you want to get married?"

"If it was up to me, I'd marry you this minute." He turned her around to face him. "I know you need time, Gina. I'm willing to wait until you're ready."

She felt the rush. Oh, she was so ready for this man. "Okay. We can talk about it. We need to talk to Zack, too. And your grandfather."

Grady grinned. "I can tell you Fletch wholeheartedly approves of us."

Gina smiled, too. "I love that man. Mainly because he raised you. He helped make you the man you are. The man I love."

"And you're the woman I love. The woman who saved me from loneliness. You were there for me when I didn't think I needed anyone. Gina, I need you in my life."

He paused and she knew he was thinking about his son.

"Oh, Grady. You've helped me through a lot of things, too. Mainly, I learned to trust." She slipped her arms around his waist. "How wonderful it is to be loved by a man who cherishes me. And you love my son." She smiled, realizing how lucky she was to find this man. "Zack's going to be so happy."

"I bet he's not nearly as happy as I am right now."

She nodded. "I think there's enough happiness to go around for all of us."

With Grady's arms wrapped around her, they looked out at the beautiful view, the site of their future home. Their new life. Together.

EPILOGUE

Two days later Saturday arrived, sunny and warm and perfect for an eight-year-old boy's birthday party. Also a great day for family, new and old. Gina felt almost giddy. Grady should be here soon and then they could announce their big news.

"Mom!" Zack came running into the house. "Did you get my cake?"

"No, Aunt Lori is bringing it," she reminded him, knowing in about thirty minutes half the town would be in her backyard for the party. They'd been lucky to find so many friends since coming to Destiny.

"Oh, I forgot," Zack said.

She hugged the little boy who suddenly looked so much older. Where had her baby gone? She got a strange feeling again, thinking about Grady and starting their new life together. Having another child. She was giddy at the thought of having Grady's baby.

"Mom. When is Grady getting here?"

She brushed his dark hair from his forehead. "Soon, he's picking someone up."

She knew Zack was eager to show off Bandit's tricks. "Come on," she said. "Let's check the tables before everyone gets here."

They walked out onto the deck to view the large

yard that had been decorated for the party. Several arrangements of balloons were tied to each fence post, and toward the back an obstacle course had been constructed late yesterday by one special man. Grady. She recalled last night, how she'd relayed her thanks to her man after Zack had gone to bed.

She could see Zack's excitement. "The obstacle course is so cool."

"Yes, it is. You're a lucky little boy, Zack Williams."

Gina twisted the large shiny pear-shaped diamond on her left hand. Grady had also surprised her when he'd slipped the engagement ring on her finger. In those stolen moments, her future husband had also proceeded to show her how much he loved her. Today was special for another reason. Grady wanted to ask Zack officially for his mother's hand before they made the announcement.

The yard gate opened and Grady walked in with Scout. Her breath caught at the sight of the tall man who was dressed in black jeans and a tan collared shirt. When he smiled at her, she saw the love shining in his eyes and nearly melted on the spot.

Zack spotted him, too. "Grady!" He went running off to him and greeted Scout. "I'm so glad you're here."

"I told you I'd come early." Grady smiled. "I brought another surprise. Someone who wants to meet you."

Grady winked at Gina and went outside the gate again, but soon returned pushing his grandfather in a wheelchair. "Zack, this is Joe Fletcher. Granddad, this is the special boy I've been telling you about."

Grady stood back and watched the two together. It was his grandfather who spoke first. "I hear you got lost in my old mine."

Zack nodded. "Yeah, but Scout found me."

"Maybe it's time I boarded that place up. Wouldn't want anyone else to get hurt."

"I think it's a cool place."

Fletch pursed his lips. "Maybe when I get out of this chair we can go up there together. I can show you where there's still some gold."

Zack's dark eyes lit up. "Really?"

Fletch nodded. "Say, I hear it's your birthday today. I got you something." He handed him the small box. "But you're gonna have to wait a little while to open it."

"Thank you. I'll put it with the other presents." He took off toward the table as Gina walked over and kissed Fletch on the cheek.

"Hello, Granddad Joe."

The older man grinned as they hugged. "There's my girl."

Grady raised an eyebrow. "Don't get any ideas, old man. She's spoken for."

Fletch waved him off and turned back to Gina. "Thanks for inviting me today."

"You're always included. You're family."

One of the many reasons Grady loved this woman— her big heart. He was one lucky man. He reached down and brushed a kiss across her lips. He couldn't help but recall their time together last night. "Hello, pretty lady." He leaned close to her ear and whispered, "I can't tell you how much I hated leaving you last night."

She looked up at him with those green eyes. "Maybe we can change that…and soon."

Before he could say any more, the boy returned with Scout. Grady stepped back from temptation. "Hey, Zack, how about we run the dogs through the obstacle course for practice?"

"Okay." Zack went to get Bandit out of the kennel.

Grady gripped Gina's hand, feeling the diamond, feeling her love, feeling her commitment to him. "Wish me luck."

"Always, but you don't need it. Zack already loves you as much as I do."

Grady looked down at his grandfather to see his smile. "I told you she was a keeper," Fletch said.

Grady motioned to Scout and together they walked off toward the edge of the yard where the course started. The boy met him there and gave the command for Bandit to sit, and then he unleashed him. Grady had Scout sit, too. "Could I talk to you, Zack, before we start?"

The boy looked worried, but nodded.

Grady knelt to be eye level. "I want to talk you about your mom." He released a breath. "You know I care about her."

Zack petted Bandit. "Yeah, I saw you kiss her."

"Does that bother you?"

The boy shook his head. "I just don't want you to hurt her like my daddy did. He was mean."

"No, Zack. That's a cowardly thing to do, especially to a woman or a child. There might be times when we disagree, but I'll never raise my hand to you or your mother. You have my word."

"I'm glad, 'cause Mom's happy now."

"And I want to make her even happier." This was harder than he thought. "I love your mother, and I want to marry her."

The boy's eyes lit up. "Really? You mean like Aunt Lori and Uncle Jace? We'd live together all the time?"

Grady smiled. "Yes. I'm building a big house so that will happen."

Zack's eyes grew larger.

Grady grew serious again. "Not only that, Zack. I want you to be my son."

"Really? You'll be my dad?"

He nodded, fighting for the right words. "As much as I love your mother, I also love you, too."

Before he could finish making his pitch, Zack had launched himself into his arms, nearly knocking him over. "I love you, too, Grady."

He hugged the boy, letting those sweet words sink in. That was when he saw Gina walk toward them. She hugged him, then her son. "So what do you think about us being a family?"

"It's cool!" Zack said. "Grady wants to be my dad." He petted Scout. "And we get to live with Scout and Bandit, too."

Grady suddenly realized how much he loved these two. "I think it's pretty cool, too." He hugged Gina to his side. "I get a wife and a son."

Zack grinned and looked up expectantly at his mother. "Mom, does that mean you're going to have a baby like Aunt Lori?"

A blush crossed Gina's face as her gaze rose to his; the love shining in their depths caused his chest to tighten with longing. He could picture Gina pregnant with his child.

She smiled. "I think that's something your new dad and I need to discuss. Alone."

Grady wished they were alone right now. "Hey, I think today is someone's birthday."

With their arms intertwined and two dogs with them, they turned back toward the house and noticed the party crowd. There was Claire and Tim Keenan, Lori, Jace and their daughter, Cassie, Justin and Morgan Hilliard and their kids. So many more gathered on the deck, but they had been giving them space. Privacy.

"I think everyone's a little curious about what's going on," Gina told him. "Maybe we should tell them."

Grady smiled. "It would be my pleasure, ma'am."

Before he could make any announcement, Zack spoke up. "Mom and Grady are getting married. And he's going to be my new dad." The boy beamed up at his parents. "This is the best birthday ever."

The crowd erupted in a round of cheers. Grady looked down at Gina and saw the love in her eyes. "How did I get so lucky?"

"Me, too."

They both had to be remembering that awful day when Zack had been kidnapped. The day one strong woman had climbed into his truck and announced she was going to get her child back. "You saved my son that day," she said.

He leaned back and brushed his mouth across hers. "No, you both saved me. I'm one lucky guy."

She smiled and his heart sang. This was their new beginning, and it was only going to get better. How could it not? He finally had everything he'd ever wanted—a home here in Destiny. And his family.

* * * * *

Mills & Boon® Hardback

February 2013

ROMANCE

Sold to the Enemy	Sarah Morgan
Uncovering the Silveri Secret	Melanie Milburne
Bartering Her Innocence	Trish Morey
Dealing Her Final Card	Jennie Lucas
In the Heat of the Spotlight	Kate Hewitt
No More Sweet Surrender	Caitlin Crews
Pride After Her Fall	Lucy Ellis
Living the Charade	Michelle Conder
The Downfall of a Good Girl	Kimberly Lang
The One That Got Away	Kelly Hunter
Her Rocky Mountain Protector	Patricia Thayer
The Billionaire's Baby SOS	Susan Meier
Baby out of the Blue	Rebecca Winters
Ballroom to Bride and Groom	Kate Hardy
How To Get Over Your Ex	Nikki Logan
Must Like Kids	Jackie Braun
The Brooding Doc's Redemption	Kate Hardy
The Son that Changed his Life	Jennifer Taylor

MEDICAL

An Inescapable Temptation	Scarlet Wilson
Revealing The Real Dr Robinson	Dianne Drake
The Rebel and Miss Jones	Annie Claydon
Swallowbrook's Wedding of the Year	Abigail Gordon

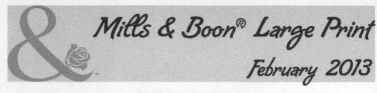

Mills & Boon® Large Print

February 2013

ROMANCE

Banished to the Harem	Carol Marinelli
Not Just the Greek's Wife	Lucy Monroe
A Delicious Deception	Elizabeth Power
Painted the Other Woman	Julia James
Taming the Brooding Cattleman	Marion Lennox
The Rancher's Unexpected Family	Myrna Mackenzie
Nanny for the Millionaire's Twins	Susan Meier
Truth-Or-Date.com	Nina Harrington
A Game of Vows	Maisey Yates
A Devil in Disguise	Caitlin Crews
Revelations of the Night Before	Lynn Raye Harris

HISTORICAL

Two Wrongs Make a Marriage	Christine Merrill
How to Ruin a Reputation	Bronwyn Scott
When Marrying a Duke...	Helen Dickson
No Occupation for a Lady	Gail Whitiker
Tarnished Rose of the Court	Amanda McCabe

MEDICAL

Sydney Harbour Hospital: Ava's Re-Awakening	Carol Marinelli
How To Mend A Broken Heart	Amy Andrews
Falling for Dr Fearless	Lucy Clark
The Nurse He Shouldn't Notice	Susan Carlisle
Every Boy's Dream Dad	Sue MacKay
Return of the Rebel Surgeon	Connie Cox

ROMANCE

Playing the Dutiful Wife	Carol Marinelli
The Fallen Greek Bride	Jane Porter
A Scandal, a Secret, a Baby	Sharon Kendrick
The Notorious Gabriel Diaz	Cathy Williams
A Reputation For Revenge	Jennie Lucas
Captive in the Spotlight	Annie West
Taming the Last Acosta	Susan Stephens
Island of Secrets	Robyn Donald
The Taming of a Wild Child	Kimberly Lang
First Time For Everything	Aimee Carson
Guardian to the Heiress	Margaret Way
Little Cowgirl on His Doorstep	Donna Alward
Mission: Soldier to Daddy	Soraya Lane
Winning Back His Wife	Melissa McClone
The Guy To Be Seen With	Fiona Harper
Why Resist a Rebel?	Leah Ashton
Sydney Harbour Hospital: Evie's Bombshell	Amy Andrews
The Prince Who Charmed Her	Fiona McArthur

MEDICAL

NYC Angels: Redeeming The Playboy	Carol Marinelli
NYC Angels: Heiress's Baby Scandal	Janice Lynn
St Piran's: The Wedding!	Alison Roberts
His Hidden American Beauty	Connie Cox

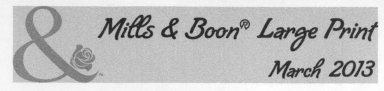

Mills & Boon® Large Print
March 2013

ROMANCE

A Night of No Return	Sarah Morgan
A Tempestuous Temptation	Cathy Williams
Back in the Headlines	Sharon Kendrick
A Taste of the Untamed	Susan Stephens
The Count's Christmas Baby	Rebecca Winters
His Larkville Cinderella	Melissa McClone
The Nanny Who Saved Christmas	Michelle Douglas
Snowed in at the Ranch	Cara Colter
Exquisite Revenge	Abby Green
Beneath the Veil of Paradise	Kate Hewitt
Surrendering All But Her Heart	Melanie Milburne

HISTORICAL

How to Sin Successfully	Bronwyn Scott
Hattie Wilkinson Meets Her Match	Michelle Styles
The Captain's Kidnapped Beauty	Mary Nichols
The Admiral's Penniless Bride	Carla Kelly
Return of the Border Warrior	Blythe Gifford

MEDICAL

Her Motherhood Wish	Anne Fraser
A Bond Between Strangers	Scarlet Wilson
Once a Playboy...	Kate Hardy
Challenging the Nurse's Rules	Janice Lynn
The Sheikh and the Surrogate Mum	Meredith Webber
Tamed by her Brooding Boss	Joanna Neil